ROGUES RAMPANT

Rogues Rampant

A Patrick Dawlish Mystery

**John Creasey *writing as*
Gordon Ashe**

OPEN ROAD
INTEGRATED MEDIA
NEW YORK

ISBN: 978-1-5040-9815-1

This edition published in 2025 by Open Road Integrated Media, Inc.
180 Maiden Lane
New York, NY 10038
www.openroadmedia.com

ROGUES RAMPANT

CHAPTER ONE

THE CUNNING OF A POLICEMAN

When Patrick Dawlish saw Superintendent Trivett of Scotland Yard approaching him in Piccadilly, some twenty yards from his Club, he thought the meeting accidental. When Trivett, after only the slightest pretence at reluctance, agreed to lunch with him, Dawlish's belief was touched by a faint doubt. The policeman was more than talkative, he was positively garrulous, leaping from subject to subject, yet showing only a facile interest in any of them.

As the Superintendent launched into yet another skimming of the respective merits of British Overseas and Pan-American airways, Dawlish finished his beer, put his tankard firmly on the table, and interrupted without apology.

'Bill,' he said, 'you should know better.'

Trivett stopped short and stared at him, perceiving a large man with powerful shoulders, flaxen hair, a broken nose which just saved him from being handsome, and a pair of dreamy blue eyes.

'Now, come!' reproached Dawlish.

Trivett looked slightly disconcerted.

'I don't see—'

'You aren't remotely interested in commercial air lines, the Chancellor of the Exchequer, where Mussolini might be hiding out, whether the children of Brazil are getting a square deal, and what the weather was like yesterday over the Straits of Dover. In short,' continued Dawlish, 'you're doing your darnedest to persuade me that our meeting was a happy accident. May I add that I'm not deceived?'

Trivett chuckled. 'All right, I'll give in,' he said. 'I thought I'd find you at the Club, that's why I came along.'

'Whatever cunning proposition you have to put up to me, I must reluctantly decline,' said Dawlish, firmly. 'Too often I have been told by policemen that I am not one of them, too often I have been warned to keep my feet out of the murky waters of crime. *Far* too often I have had to defend myself vigorously, denying that I have any interest in police work, in crime, or in anything except a quiet life. I do not want to spend any part of the next four days keeping my eyes open for the benefit of a policeman.'

'My, my. What a man for words and phrases!' said Trivett, amiably. 'As a matter of fact, Pat—I hoped to get you curious, but since you're forcing the issue—'

'Not I,' declared Dawlish, 'I'm evading it by turning the proposition down. Even if I felt like keeping a weather-eye open for you, after your base deception I'd prefer to be lazy.'

'Tell me,' said Trivett abruptly: 'Have you any special plans for the next few days?'

'Indeed I have. Whitehall is again seething with rumour, which means that all of us will be at action stations for the next month or so. Then we'll get general leave, only to be recalled after a couple of hours. The one thing I have come to suspect is a dearth of rumours. If there are none, then trouble's brewing.'

'I phoned your office this morning,' Trivett said drily, 'and was informed that you wouldn't be in again until Wednesday. It's now Friday.'

Dawlish grinned.

'That's the trouble with policemen, they can't help snooping.' He paused, then added: 'I suppose you'd better unburden yourself now, as later, for I see it in your eye that you intend to do so. Carry on.'

Trivett gave a sigh of relief.

'Good man! Do you know of a place called Terne?'

Dawlish raised an eyebrow.

'I haven't been there, but I've certainly read of it, and no later than in the *Sunday Cry* of last week. A little, out-of-the-way town on the edge of Salisbury Plain. Isolated, unremarkable, and probably unpleasant.'

Trivett smiled: 'So you know about the case?'

'Certainly not. I merely happened to read that the *Cry* for some reason that's escaped me, had sent a reporter to inquire into the whereabouts of a lovely housekeeper. The third, I believe.'

With a sudden, boyish gesture he tapped Trivett on the knee. 'You don't want me to present myself as the would-be fourth housekeeper, by any chance, do you?'

To his surprise, Trivett did not appear to think the idea funny.

'As a matter of fact—' began the policeman, and then broke off. 'It doesn't matter,' he muttered. 'Just an idea, and I'm not serious about it. I don't mean that I wouldn't be glad if you could go down to Terne, but—'

Dawlish interrupted.

'You look like a fifth-former with a guilty secret, or a lifelong friend trying to borrow yet another fiver. Confound it, you've even gone red!'

'Er—just an idea,' mumbled Trivett. He drew out his wallet and extracted a newspaper cutting; smoothing it out, he passed it to Dawlish, who read:

WANTED at once. Housekeeper to widower. Large Country house. 3 maids kept. Excellent salary. No experience necessary. Apply: Mr. Clive Dickerson, Wood Grange, Terne, Dorset.

'Hum,' said Dawlish. 'When did this appear?'

'On Monday, in the local daily paper,' said Trivett. 'As an advertisement for these days there's nothing surprising in it. What is surprising, is its insertion at all. I would have expected Dickerson to tone the advert down, even if he didn't cancel it altogether,' went on Trivett judicially. 'It's an evening paper, and he would have had ample time. Instead, he adopted an attitude of "confound the lot of them" and let it go. Sunday's *Cry* was pretty outspoken, and most people in Dickerson's position would have considered an action for libel, or at least made some representation to the Press.'

'There hasn't been much time,' Dawlish pointed out.

'Time enough. As a matter of fact, Pat,' Trivett continued a little sheepishly, 'I've had a sergeant down there. The *Cry* was delivered to the house, deliberately, to make sure that Dickerson didn't miss it. From his servants' comments, I gather that he was highly amused.'

'Curious,' conceded Dawlish, thoughtfully.

'That's what I thought. Taking the facts as they are, he has had three housekeepers, all youngish and attractive women, and all three wives of men in the Forces. As far as I can gather, after working for a week or two, all three have disappeared. The husband of the last of them, a man named Bryant, came home on leave and made inquiries. He didn't get any satisfaction out of Dickerson, so he went to the local police. He didn't get any satisfaction out of them either, so he came to us. As it happened, the local people had reported the first two missing housekeepers and the fact that Dickerson has a peculiar reputation down at Terne—nothing very much to go on, I'm afraid,' Trivett added. 'Mainly that the locals are scared of him.'

'Scared?' repeated Dawlish, as if he had not heard right.

'Apparently they are frightened of him and of Wood Grange. The servants he's had from the nearest village won't stay, so he's imported some from further afield. He pays exceptionally high wages so he keeps the main staff, although he can't get local help.'

'Hum,' said Dawlish.

'Between you and me,' said Trivett, 'I asked Dippy Fowler, of the *Cry*, to go down there.'

'*You* asked the *Cry* to do that story?' exclaimed Dawlish.

'Oh, no! I simply told Fowler that he might find something interesting at Terne. I know the *Cry* will often go pretty near the bone and I thought if he would dish up a potent article it might provoke Dickerson into some kind of retort. Instead, it appears to have amused the gentleman, and stimulated him into inserting an advertisement for yet a fourth housekeeper. I thought if you had a few days to spare you might like to go down and make a few inquiries, and let me know what you think about it. Nothing more than that,' added Trivett blandly. 'Of course, if you—'

'I hand it to you,' said Dawlish, with a reluctant grin.

'What the dickens are you talking about?' demanded Trivett, a little too innocently.

'You know very well what I'm talking about,' growled Dawlish. 'You're pretending that your sole idea was to interest me, but you're hoping that I might encourage Felicity to apply for the job. Where are your morals? Where's your sense of friendship?'

'Felicity?' cried Trivett. 'Why, I didn't give her a thought! But now you mention it—'

'I knew it!' said Dawlish, 'but the answer is no, Bill. Firmly, finally, and once and for all. That is,' added Dawlish, after a pause, 'unless you've something very much stronger to offer as an inducement. The disappearance of charming housekeepers, disturbing though it must be, doesn't attract me. Felicity might think my interest was not impersonal, anyhow.'

'Oh, no, she wouldn't,' said Trivett, confidently. 'I telephoned her this morning and told her that if she could help and you cared to slip down to Terne, it would be a load off my mind.' He grinned disarmingly at Dawlish's astonished expression. 'I told her that I didn't feel like putting it up to you without first seeing what she thought of it, and if she wasn't too shocked by the idea, I felt sure you'd come in.'

'You are no longer a friend of mine,' said Dawlish, coldly. 'What did she say?'

Trivett hid a look of triumph. He knew both Dawlish and Felicity well, and had some idea that much of Dawlish's reluctance to engage in dangerous activities was due to Felicity's usually obdurate attitude towards such sorties unless they were unavoidable. By first approaching Felicity he had proved how deeply he and the police were concerned by the curious disappearances of the housekeepers of Wood Grange. He had built up his case with admirable care, showing that he had not only worked through the local police and one of the Yard's sergeants, but also through Dippy Fowler, of the *Cry*. That Fowler, the Terne police, a Yard man and Trivett could find no way of taking action, and yet remained interested enough to want to find out more, would prove a tempting bait for Dawlish—whose most likely objective, the reluctance of Felicity, had already been overcome.

To say 'no' would be for obstinacy's sake alone; Trivett knew that, as well as Dawlish, who, smiling with deceptive mildness, said that he would think it over.

Trivett added helpfully, that if the thought of a train journey put Dawlish off, he could probably arrange some petrol. If nothing else had, this offer assured Dawlish of the importance of the proposed mission.

CHAPTER TWO

FELICITY

Dawlish's fiancée and an officer in the A.T.S., Felicity Deverall, had been staying with friends for the first two days of her leave. Had Dawlish been free, he would have spent them with her, but a furious burst of activity at his Whitehall office had kept him at the desk until an hour or so before he had left for his Club and the encounter with Trivett.

Dawlish's flat in Jermyn Street having been reduced to rubble during the days of the blitz, he now shared one with his friend, Tim Jeremy. The flat shortage being acute Felicity, too, and a friend of hers, when on leave, joined them. All were in the Services, none of them sure where they would be stationed at any particular time, so each had a key of the flat and used it, when on leave.

This working arrangement had been in operation for so long that only when he met a disapproving relative did Dawlish realise that it might be regarded as being unconventional.

It was just such a relative—the hawk-eyed Honourable David Clynton-Green—Dawlish now encountered, Trivett having left him, in the smoking room of his Club.

In vain Dawlish attempted to escape behind a barrage of the opened *Times*. Clynton-Green stalked him down, and stood regarding him. It was clear that a homily was on the way. It might concern any one of a number of misdemeanours, for Dawlish's activities were not approved by his relatives unanimously, and he knew that Clynton-Green considered that he should be on active service, rather than at Whitehall; an opinion his nephew fervently shared.

'Well, Patrick,' said Clynton-Green, taking the cigar from his lips and eyeing it speculatively. 'It's a funny thing that I should run across you—very funny. We were talking about you only last night.'

'Oh, were you?' asked Dawlish, realising his chances of stemming the coming lecture were small indeed. 'How is Aunt Cris?'

'She is very well, thank you,' said Clynton-Green. 'How is that young woman of yours?'

'Nasty ring about "that young woman",' said Dawlish, tolerantly. 'I hope you're not going to—'

'Patrick,' interrupted Clynton-Green, 'you have known her for three years, perhaps a little more. I have met her on a number of occasions and I must admit—I *gladly* admit—that she is a most charmin' gal. Charmin'. But are you being fair to her, my boy? I ask you to ask yourself—*are* you being fair to her?'

'In about five minutes, uncle, if I let you go on, you'll ask me why I don't marry her.'

'Now, now! Don't take offence, my boy!' Clynton-Green leant forward earnestly. 'I like your frankness, Patrick—always have admired it, as a matter of fact. Don't say that I was always what I should have been when I was young'—he looked positively waggish—'but it remains a fact, you know, that people talk. I don't give a damn what they say about you, but—well, you know what I mean, my boy.' He paused, but at sight of Dawlish's forbidding frown went on hastily: 'Now don't misunderstand me, Patrick! Nothin' would give me more pleasure than to hear that you were goin' to get married. *Charmin'* gal, I've always said so. But—'

'In our own good time, we will get married,' said Dawlish. He paused, feeling more angry than the circumstances warranted, perhaps because there was some slight justification for the other's attitude, then went on: 'However, you can tell my anxious relations that the Jermyn Street flat is no more an abode of the loose-living than Clynton House or Pitcairn Lodge.'

'My dear boy! I never thought it was, but—'

'Yes, I know—people talk,' said Dawlish, a trifle bitterly.

Not without embarrassment, Clynton-Green puffed at his cigar.

'I'm very glad to hear it, Patrick—not a pleasant job, you know, being spokesman in such a matter. After all, the head of the family—some responsibility—if your father were alive I wouldn't dream of interfering. Your aunt—' his voice trailed off, and then bellowed out with a sudden spurt of energy.

'Patrick, why *don't* you get married?'

Dawlish eyed him steadily.

'Do I have to say that there's a war on?'

'Yes, yes, I know, my boy, but—'

'Personally, I don't like the thought of Felicity being widowed,' said Dawlish, 'and I keep hoping that the Powers that Be will send me abroad. Oh, I know all the arguments—' he stopped, abruptly. 'I'm getting quite heated, aren't I?'

Clynton-Green gave a slow, charming smile.

'Yes, Patrick, you are,' he admitted, 'and I like you for it. Now listen to me! I'm not speaking for the family now, but as an old man who *has* seen a little more of life than you. Don't wait for the last trump; it might never sound. Wasn't really sure what you felt, before, but—if you're both of a mind and want to get married, don't let some silly prejudice on your part stop you. High-sounding motives are all very well, my boy! but unless I'm making a great mistake, *you're* the only one who feels like it, women don't, you know. Perhaps you think you're being fair to Felicity, but you might be wrong. No offence, I hope?'

Dawlish's lips began to curve.

'No-o,' he said slowly, 'and it's just possible that you might be right.'

'You ask Felicity!' urged Clynton-Green. 'Talk it over with her, my boy. I—good gracious me, what's the time? Half past two!'

He bounded from his chair, shook hands warmly, and made for the door, in what he obviously considered to be the appropriate moment. Dawlish watched him go, smiling ruefully. There was more in Uncle David than he had admitted before—and the old boy might be right.

He wondered how long it would take to get a licence.

There was no harm in finding out. Quickly he rose to his feet and hurried to the telephone. He called Peter Fraser, a cleric of his acquaintance. Fraser took the inquiry in a matter-of-fact way and assured Dawlish that if he really wanted a special licence it could be obtained and he could get married the next day, but it would be less trouble to apply for a licence that day and get married three days later.

'Right. If I ring you again later, can you arrange for the one-day licence?'

'Certainly. Are you being moved overseas?'

'No,' said Dawlish, 'but—'

He paused, for it was the first time since he had seen Uncle David that he had remembered Trivett's problem and the fact that Felicity had already given virtual consent to a visit to Terne.

Confound it, not on their honeymoon! He said hastily that he had a job on hand which he had not expected, promised to ring through again, and then looked at his watch. It was ten minutes to three. Felicity would probably be at the flat by four o'clock. He reached it just after three o'clock.

Looking about him, he came to the conclusion that the rooms looked forlorn and unoccupied. He laid a small table for tea; that helped, but did not satisfy him. With his head on one side, he debated what was missing, deciding in a burst of inspiration that the explanation was—*flowers*! By then it was a quarter to four; he had fifteen minutes in which to put matters right. He hurried out, and was fortunate in finding a hawker with a barrow-load of daffodils. He bought half a dozen bundles and carefully carried the dripping armful back to the flat. Before he could find his key, the door opened. Felicity stood there, laughing and welcoming.

'Felicity!' Dawlish dropped the flowers, regardless of where they fell. 'By George, it's good to see you!'

He seized her in a bear-like hug.

'Oughtn't we to pick them up?' asked Felicity a few minutes later.

Dawlish grinned sheepishly. 'I suppose so—' They were bending down, their heads close together, retrieving the flowers. 'Have we enough vases for them?'

'Well,' said Felicity, 'we could put them in the sink.'

'Sink?' ejaculated Dawlish. They both looked up at the same moment. 'Sink?' echoed Dawlish, and then saw her lips quivering with suppressed laughter. 'How *practical* can women be! Where is their romance?' He picked up what remained of the flowers from the floor, and festooned ridiculously with their bright blooms, staggered into the kitchen.

When he returned to the living-room, Felicity was still standing where he had left her, her eyes so bright that he saw that if she was not crying, she was very near to it. He stared aghast.

'Fel! What is it?' His mind was suddenly filled with forebodings, he experienced a great fear; *why* should she be crying? 'Fel!' he said again. 'What is it? Fel, what is it?'

CHAPTER THREE

FELICITY ASKS 'WHY?'

'N-nothing,' said Felicity, in an uncertain voice. She dabbed her eyes, and went on in a more controlled voice. 'Darling, I know I'm a fool, but I couldn't help it. Seeing you coming in with your arms loaded with flowers—what on earth made you do it?'

Dawlish said shyly: 'I—I don't know. I wanted to celebrate. I mean, leave together for the first time for over a year, no one else here, and—well, the flat looked unlived-in, you know what I mean. It wasn't good enough.' He grinned, boyishly. 'I was at the Club and after Trivett had said his piece I met—'

'Oh!' ejaculated Felicity, in a changed voice. 'So you're going to Terne and this is—a peace offering?'

'Peace offering?' repeated Dawlish. She seemed suddenly a long way removed from him. '*Peace* offering? Stiffen my Aunt Maria, no! I don't much care whether we go to Terne or not, I'd practically decided to tell Trivett that I'd changed my mind.' He put out a hand and gripped her shoulder. 'Fel, I was telling you—I met Uncle David.'

This time her expression changed to one of complete bewilderment.

'Oh, damn it all!' roared Dawlish. 'The old boy was on the usual rampage. This flat, conventions, why don't we make up our minds? Quite human, actually. Told him why we didn't—er—why I wouldn't—you know—and he as good as called me a fool. He convinced me that I had been a blind idiot for the last couple of years. Home truths from Uncle David! I—' he stopped again. 'Fel, you've been right and I've only just realised it,' he went on. 'I phoned Peter Fraser, who said we *can* arrange everything by tomorrow. Need we wait? I mean—you haven't changed your mind, you don't think—'

'Pat!' cried Felicity.

Fully twenty minutes later they made some tea, forgot to drink it, moved about the flat as in a dream, Dawlish unaware that he was grinning inanely, Felicity looking at him as if she were seeing him for the first time. They had agreed that three days was far too long, if Peter Fraser could make the necessary arrangements for a licence by the following day, it would not be a day too soon. They walked on air.

At half past six, after Dawlish had telephoned Fraser again, there was a ring at the front door. They said: 'I'll go,' together, and actually stood by the open door, side by side, in startled and mutual amazement, at the trim figure of Trivett.

Trivett was quick to offer his felicitations. If he showed that the sudden change of programme disappointed him because it affected the prospect of solving the mystery of Mr. Clive Dickerson, that was only to be expected. He covered it well, agreeing to be one of the witnesses and suggested that his wife might be the other. If Felicity would like to spend the night at his home, his wife would be delighted. His offer was accepted warmly. Not once, before he rose to go half an hour after his arrival, did he refer to Terne.

Politely, Dawlish murmured:

'No new discoveries about *l'affaire* Dickerson, I suppose?'

'You don't want to talk about that, now,' said Trivett bravely.

'*Are* there any new developments?' insisted Felicity.

'We-ell—there's something that might become one. A woman's body has been found in the river just north of Terne, dressed in the clothes of one of the housekeepers. No evidence of foul play, and no sure identification, but—still, you needn't worry about that, now—'

Dawlish was looking at Felicity, Felicity at Dawlish.

'Do you think we might have helped?'

'Oh, I don't suppose you would have made much difference.' Trivett shook hands with Dawlish, kissed Felicity—'I claim the privilege,' he said lightly, and let himself out.

Dawlish and Felicity washed up the tea things in silence. Twice Dawlish began to speak and then said that it did not matter. Three times Felicity began: 'Pat, do you—' only to break off. Back in the living-room, Dawlish took the plunge at last.

'I wonder if we've really damned Bill's hopes.' When Felicity said nothing he went on: 'I've never known him go to so much trouble to get us interested.'

'Well?' said Felicity.

'Honeymoon?' asked Dawlish.

'We could have a few days in the country,' said Felicity reflectively.

'We *will* have! The thing is—Bill half-promised some petrol. Train travelling is grim, these days. I mean, if we headed for Terne, we *could* have a look round, as a salve to our conscience for using his petrol.'

'It's a hundred miles to Terne,' mused Felicity. 'If the weather holds it would be a glorious run.' She considered. 'We could use the little car, it wouldn't take so much petrol.'

Dawlish said: 'Fel, do *you* want to go?'

'We-ell,' admitted Felicity. 'I'd rather be away from London for what few days we have, it would be more pleasant to travel by road, and Terne—have you ever been there?'

'No.'

'It's a sixteenth-century town, and quite the loveliest I know,' said Felicity. 'At the *George*—'

'What and where is the *George*?'

'A hotel just off the High Street. I stayed there with my mother once, and I thought Terne was the ideal place for a country holiday.' She ruffled Dawlish's hair, absently—'I'd rather stay there than anywhere else and if you *could* help—but do you want to?'

Dawlish said: 'I feel rather guilty at letting Bill down.'

Felicity stood up and smoothed her skirt. 'Well, that settles it. Phone the *George*, Pat! If there's a room, we'll go. If there isn't, we'll call it the finger of fate and go somewhere else,' said Felicity. 'Shall we?'

'We will!'

It took him twenty minutes to find out the number of the *George* and a further ten to get through, but after that, everything went smoothly enough. The room was booked for the following night and five days thereafter. Dawlish gave his name and said that they would arrive sometime before dinner the following evening. He rang off, and smiled ecstatically at Felicity.

'So that's that! Darling, all we've got to do is to pack some clothes and phone Bill and Uncle David.'

Uncle David was momentarily bereft of words at the news and then grew garrulous in his congratulations and promised to be at the church; there were, he said, formalities which he could best handle. He talked down all of Dawlish's protests, assuring him that it would be no trouble. As he was about to ring off, Dawlish heard an interruption by his aunt.

He was tempted to ring off, expecting to be forced to receive yet more congratulations, which would keep him at the phone for half an hour, but his uncle's sobering voice forestalled him.

'A little family news your aunt thinks I should tell you,' he went on not too happily. 'It's about Sheila, who of course, is most upset, although I don't mind admitting that I didn't think James was *quite* the man for her.'

'Sheila?' echoed Dawlish; she was his cousin, but not a daughter of the Clynton-Greens. 'James—oh, I remember—in the R.A.F., wasn't he?' For the first time he felt doubtful of the wisdom of his sudden decision to marry. Here was an example of the thing he feared—except that Sheila had not been married. Memories of Sheila and her James came to him with greater clarity. Sheila had refused quite a few eligible young men and then fallen for a not too prepossessing young man in R.A.F. blue, later sent to Canada.

'I think it was largely Sheila's fault, mind you,' went on Undle David, 'she would never fix a date, and you can delay these things too long, my boy!' He chuckled, roguishly. 'I hardly expected him to marry someone else, all the same. Sheila is rather depressed, as you can imagine, it's a good thing that she has the business to look after.'

'Business,' thought Dawlish, and remembered that Sheila had a hat shop in Brook Street.

An idea burst upon him, dazzling in its brightness. *No* one could act the part of a housekeeper better than Sheila.

'Is she there now?' asked Dawlish, eagerly.

'No, Patrick, she's spending the night at her flat, over the shop, you know. I think she might have been wiser to have come here, but—oh, well! Young people always know best—or think they do.'

'Too bad,' said Dawlish, brightly, 'but perhaps you were as

right about James as you were about me!' He rang off quickly, and looked up to find Felicity regarding him with appraising eyes and a speculative smile.

'Darling, I *think* you've had a bright idea.'

'Well, as a matter of fact, I *have*,' said Dawlish, suddenly serious. 'You haven't met my cousin Sheila, have you? Nice girl. Engaged to someone who's just married someone else.' He looked ingenuously into Felicity's eyes—'if she *could* be persuaded to come down to Terne—' he paused.

'Would she?' asked Felicity. 'Apply for the job, I mean?'

'I wouldn't be surprised,' said Dawlish. 'It's the kind of thing that might appeal to her, and she'll be feeling at a loose end and all that, and might do something she wouldn't look at in normal times.'

'Why don't you go to see her?'

Dawlish grew thoughtful. 'Of course, she'd have to travel by train, it wouldn't do for us to be seen arriving together. In a town like Terne rumour travels fast and Dickerson would probably know of it before we could turn round. I will put it to her!'

He telephoned Sheila. Would she be in if he went to her Brook Street flat at half past nine?

'Or, better still,' he amended, 'come round for a spot of dinner with Felicity and me—I'm having something sent up from the restaurant.'

'I've nothing much to do,' Sheila admitted; she had a husky voice and spoke rather abruptly, 'but if you're trying to take my mind off—'

She arrived at half past eight, meticulously dressed, very much on her guard against sympathy, and firmly prepared to put gloom behind her.

Once greetings were over, Dawlish told her the story, going fully into the *Cry* article and not failing to mention the body found in the river near Terne.

'Pat thought you might like to help by applying for the job,' Felicity said a little diffidently, 'but now I've heard it put so bluntly, it doesn't seem such a good idea.'

Sheila smiled. 'The chief snag that I can see is the possibility that Dickerson has already engaged someone,' she said calmly. 'If he hasn't—'

'You'll try it!' exclaimed Dawlish. 'Good girl! Supposing you phone Dickerson from here, and find out?'

CHAPTER FOUR

MORE BRIGHT IDEAS

It was an evening when many things went smoothly. For instance, directory inquiries gave Dawlish Dickerson's telephone number quickly and there was no delay on the call to Terne 56. Sheila asked to speak to Mr. Dickerson and then waited, while Dawlish slipped into the other room where he had an extension telephone. Dawlish hardly knew what kind of voice to expect; certainly Dickerson's surprised him, for the only word to describe it was 'hearty'; yet it was a likeable voice and travelled clearly.

'Clive Dickerson speaking,' he said. 'Who is that?'

'My name is Lynd,' said Sheila. 'Good evening, Mr. Dickerson. I have just seen a copy of the *Dayshire Echo* and read your advertisement for a housekeeper. Are you suited yet?'

Dawlish's grip on the telephone tightened; only then did he realise how much the answer mattered.

'No,' said Dickerson, briefly.

'I am speaking from London,' said Sheila. 'I could come for an interview tomorrow or the next day, provided—'

'My dear Miss Lynd,' Dickerson nearly chuckled, 'you are about to refer to expenses, I take it. There will be no problem there. I will pay them, whether we come to an arrangement or not.' Again there was a slight suggestion of a laugh in his voice; Dawlish found it irritating. 'Have you held any similar post, Miss Lynd?'

'I have assisted my parents,' Sheila said crisply, 'and I have been in business for myself for some time.'

'Admirable!' exclaimed Dickerson. 'The best train from London in the morning is the ten-thirty from Waterloo, Miss Lynd. Travel first class. You should be here soon after two o'clock and I will arrange to have some lunch kept for you.'

'Please don't bother about that,' said Sheila, quickly.

'Oh, but I insist!'

'Very well,' said Sheila. 'Thank you.'

'Tomorrow afternoon, then, at two o'clock,' said Dickerson. 'You will have to get a taxi from Terne station, it is two miles from there to Wood Grange. Should we come to terms it may be necessary to make an arrangement with the Employment Exchange, but that can be done, don't allow it to deter you. Good night, Miss Lynd!'

Dickerson rang off, the faint echo of laughter still in his voice. Dawlish replaced the extension telephone and walked, frowning, into the other room.

'Well, what did you make of him?' Felicity asked.

'Odd customer,' said Dawlish. 'No doubt about that.'

'*Very* friendly,' said Sheila. 'Remarkably friendly, in fact, and very generous!' She laughed, lightly. 'Pat, I don't know why I've let you talk me into this!'

'Now, come!' protested Dawlish, 'it's of your own free will, you can't deny that. But—' he paused. 'You know, it isn't too late to back out. We don't want to fish you out of the river, you know. I'm beginning to wonder whether—'

'Nonsense!' exclaimed Sheila. 'At least I can go through with the interview, I haven't committed myself to anything else yet.

It's time I was off,' she added, glancing at her watch. 'I'll have to pack a few things, for I've a feeling that he'll want me to start forthwith!' She laughed again, and went into Felicity's bedroom to put on her coat. Felicity followed her. 'Sheila, do you really want to go to Terne?' she asked.

Sheila spoke quickly.

'I do, yes. My outraged vanity needs some outlet. Adventure spiced with danger is just the thing. You've worked with Pat yourself, haven't you?'

'Ye-es,' admitted Felicity, slowly, 'and I haven't always liked it. He not only takes enormous risks but gets absolutely absorbed in what he's doing. In a way, I wish it hadn't worked out like this. Oh, I know I could have prevented it, but if we'd gone somewhere else it would have kept popping in and out of his mind, so—' she broke off with a smile.

Sheila kissed Felicity lightly. 'Good night, my dear!'

An hour later, having left Felicity at Trivett's Chelsea home, Dawlish went round to his garage. He found that the night mechanic, according to his instructions, had tried the engine and serviced the car, which he pronounced good for any distance.

The telephone was ringing as Dawlish walked up the stairs to his flat; it was a distant relative, who had 'just heard the glad news'. Dawlish made suitable responses; in the next half an hour he grew weary and ill-tempered, for the telephone rang five times, always for the same reason. It was half past twelve before he got to bed, the affair of Dickerson relegated to a very obscure corner of his mind.

The morning brought seven telegrams of congratulation, two bills, and the newspaper—at which Dawlish no more than glanced. While he was at breakfast Trivett arrived.

'That woman, Pat,' he murmured, mildly.

'Eh? What woman?'

'The body in the river,' said Trivett, patiently. 'I'm sorry to have to talk about it, but you ought to be primed. I've written up a report on all I know and all the local police have discovered—it doesn't amount to much, mind you, but—'

'Does it say why you're so interested?' demanded Dawlish, pausing in the middle of shaving.

'I've told you that,' said Trivett, a shade too quickly.

'So,' thought Dawlish, 'you're keeping something back, as well as I!' Aloud, he said amiably: 'All right, I'll take your word for it. What about the corpse in the river? Was it one of the housekeepers?'

Trivett said: 'No, but wearing the clothes of Hilda Bryant, the last of the three. I've given you all the details in the report.'

Dawlish declared that it was a very rum business indeed; then, as he was knotting his tie—he suddenly stopped and swung round on Trivett.

'Good Lord! Bill, I've forgotten the ring! What's the time?' It was just past ten o'clock and he was due at the church at eleven.

Trivett smiled complacently.

'Felicity reminded me before I left,' he said. 'She tried one of Grace's rings for size and I slipped into a shop on my way here. Think yourself lucky I'm a policeman,' he added, 'trained for every contingency.'

He held out a platinum wedding ring for Dawlish's inspection.

'Nice work!' he said admiringly. 'Thanks, Bill. I'll square up with you afterwards.'

There followed a trying hour, for at the church there was a crowd of relatives and friends and newspaper reporters, but the service went without a hitch. Stoically Dawlish endured the kissing and the handshaking and the levelling of cameras.

Afterwards he said that it was like a dream. Someone raised a cheer, two photographers took last minute pictures, the engine stalled, but he drove off at last. Safely round the corner into Hyde Park, he pulled up. Drawing a deep breath he looked at Felicity.

'Good morning, darling!' he said. 'We're *married*! We're actually *married*!'

They were both laughing when he started the car again and began the journey to Terne.

CHAPTER FIVE

THE TOWN OF TERNE

Sheila Lynd alighted from the train at Terne and no porter being available, carried her heavy suitcase towards the main exit. As she went into the station yard, her heart dropped, for there was a queue for taxis and already the suitcase was weighing her down. She took her place at the end of the queue, and immediately an oldish man wearing a chauffeur's uniform approached her.

'Excuse me, Ma'am, are you Miss Lynd?'

'Yes.' Sheila was startled.

'Mr. Dickerson sent me for you, Ma'am.'

He took the case and carried it to the other side of the yard where a large Austin was waiting.

The development was not surprising, in view of Dickerson's conversation on the telephone, and yet Sheila was puzzled by the trouble the man was taking. Few prospective employers would hire a taxi for such a purpose. Shrugging her shoulders, she sat back in the tonneau as the man put the car in gear and drove off.

Skirting the town, they drove along a wide, tree-lined thoroughfare and on into fairly open country. Unexpectedly, the driver slowed down at a gate-way which appeared to lead to nowhere, but actually led to Wood Grange.

Sturdy shrubs, backed by limes and chestnuts, dotted the grass-land. The drive was narrow but well tended, with banks of flowers on either side, leading up to a house set high above the river.

Sheila felt an excitement which only the unexpectedness of the adventure could have induced, for the house, of reddish-brown brick, was charming but by no means out of the ordinary. French windows opened from a room on one side.

As she stepped from the car, tension, suspicion, and vague impressions disappeared. She stood still, staring from the drive towards Terne and the country about it. The Grange was perhaps a thousand feet above sea level and the land fell abruptly away from it; the gradual ascent had not made her realise the height to which the taxi had climbed.

The town was no more than two miles away, clearly visible in the afternoon sun. Through its centre flowed the River Tan, a silvery ribbon twisting and turning inconsequentially, looking now broad, now narrow, until it was lost to view.

For the first time a darkling thought entered Sheila's mind; somewhere in that river the body of a woman had been found—clad in the clothes of a housekeeper from this house; she did not yet know that the body had been that of someone so far unidentified, not a servant of Clive Dickerson's.

She was aware of a soft footstep, a faint noise on the gravel.

'Favourably impressed, Miss Lynd?'

Sheila looked at the man standing beside her.

She knew from his voice that it was Dickerson. He was tall, well-built, and well-dressed—and extremely handsome. Fair and bearded, he looked to be a man of perhaps forty-five or fifty.

She answered him pleasantly, noting, when he spoke again,

that his voice held the same heartiness she had heard the previous evening.

'That's good,' he declared. 'It's always important to like a thing at first sight.' Just as on the previous night there seemed to be an echo of laughter in his voice, as if everything were wonderful and the slightest thing amused him. 'Although I say it myself, there aren't many lovelier spots in England—in the world, for that matter! I spent three years looking for it.'

'Indeed,' said Sheila.

'I looked south, west, east, and north!' Dickerson continued, gaily, 'but I didn't find anything so perfect as Terne, or the view from this hill. I built the house myself, ten years ago—you'll find it's remarkably easy to run, remarkably! But you must be tired and hungry, I'll take you in.'

A little nervously Sheila stepped over the threshold. The hall, stretching from the front to the back of the house, was wide, bright with the sun, and well-furnished. A narrow staircase led upwards. By the foot of the stairs stood a little, middle-aged woman in a cap and apron.

'Now!' Dickerson spoke briskly. 'Maude will show you about, Miss Lynd, and I don't propose to talk business until after you've had a wash and some lunch—or lunch first, just as you like. Look after Miss Lynd, Maude!' He nodded to the maid, then again to Sheila, and walked quickly up the stairs.

Sheila looked at Maude, whose face was expressionless; she was a faded little creature, with mournful eyes and thin lips, her mouth deeply indented at the corners.

'I think I'll wash first,' said Sheila.

'Yes'm. Y'room's upstairs'm.' Maude spoke with an accent which Sheila could not place, but she was less interested in placing it than in the word 'y'room'; *her* room. Dickerson, then, was sure that she would stay. She followed the maid upstairs to a wide landing. Opening a door she stood aside for Sheila to enter. Her eyes followed the younger woman as she stepped through—waiting, perhaps, for a sign of surprise or pleasure, for one wall seemed to be all window, and through it the view was even better than from the drive.

The room itself was large and well-furnished, with two doors leading from it; Sheila could just glimpse a luxuriously appointed bathroom. She made no comment, conscious of an impression that the woman was weighing her up and would soon report her reactions to Dickerson; she had the idea that a single false word might be fatal.

'Where is lunch served?' she asked.

'Downstairs, m'm.'

'I will be down in ten minutes. Thank you, Maude.' She smiled but left the maid in no doubt that she wanted her to go; she thought the little woman went reluctantly.

When the door closed, Sheila turned the key. She could not understand why she was so nervous. This place was a dream—better than anything of its kind she had ever seen, perfect in appointment and taste; no one who wanted a housekeeper's job would fail to see that it was a job in a thousand—at first sight, at least.

She washed quickly, ran a comb through her hair, and dallied with the idea of unpacking and making a quick change. She dismissed it; if she put on a frock she would give the impression that she had come prepared to stay.

Lunch was a cold one, excellently prepared, with copies of *The Times* and the *Daily Mirror* beside her plate. Sheila helped herself to the food with appetite and pleasure, then, sitting back, opened the *Daily Mirror*.

Rigid with astonishment she stared at the picture of Dickerson smiling out of the middle page!

She read the accompanying article avidly; it was a rehash of Dippy Fowler's in the *Cry* and told her everything she had learned from Dawlish. The facts leapt baldly out of the page. In the past four months three women, employed as housekeepers by Clive Dickerson, had disappeared. On the next column, as if running a different story, was an account of the woman whose body had been found in the river. Then followed a row of photographs—the three housekeepers, all of them pleasant-looking, and, Sheila judged, about her own age.

Her appetite had gone; she turned from the table and rang a small handbell. After only a brief delay Maude brought in the coffee. She glanced at Sheila, who was not sure whether the glance was one of veiled hostility or simple curiosity.

The coffee was good, both hot and strong and Sheila drank eagerly as Maude began to pile dishes on to a trolley. She was quick and efficient—and yet she seemed to linger. Two or three times Sheila thought that she was going to speak, but each time she changed her mind. She began to wheel the trolley towards the door, and then walked quickly back across the room. Sheila was startled; the little woman's face held an expression that was difficult to understand but which might have been fear.

'Y'won't tell the Boss I spoke to you?' The eyes *were* frightened, the woman's hand was unsteady and she made the words an appeal.

'You haven't said—' began Sheila.

'I'm going to!' the maid exclaimed, and drew in a deep breath. 'I can't stand by an' see yer stay. Don't *stay*, m'm! Never mind what he offers yer, don't stay! See?'

Maude turned abruptly, opened the door and trundled out with the trolley; the door closed with a snap and Sheila stared, unseeing, into the garden.

She sat for a long time, letting the coffee get cold.

Soon afterwards the door opened again. Maude stood there impassively. Dickerson would see Miss Lynd now, if she were ready.

CHAPTER SIX

SHEILA TELLS A STORY

Dawlish hummed loudly as he scattered his belongings about the large, low-ceilinged room at the *George*. Sheila and Dickerson were not altogether forgotten, but they did not make a very deep impression on his mind.

He and Felicity had reached Terne just after four o'clock, had tea and gone for a walk in the wooded country just outside the town. Now he was unpacking while Felicity was taking a bath.

He felt hungry, relaxed, and thoroughly contented. The M.G. had given no trouble, the road had been practically empty, they had happened upon a charming place for lunch—and he had signed the register for 'Mr. and Mrs. Patrick Dawlish'.

Suddenly, he stiffened and went nearer the window, for a voice had uttered the name 'Dickerson'. The window overlooked the yard of the *George* and bending forward he saw a group of men washing down a governess cart.

'Saw William meself, this afternoon, and he told me. Very handsome woman, he said, like all of them. *I* wouldn't take a job at the Grange, that I wouldn't, not for a fortune.'

'You're soft,' declared his companion. 'Pays well, that Dickerson, don't he?' That appeared to be unanswerable. 'Well, there y'ar! Lot o' silly wimmin's talk, *that's* what I say. If he was to offer me a job, I'd take it.'

'Well, I know one thing—I wouldn't let a girl o' mine work at the Grange, and that's that!'

'Same 'ere,' said an unknown.

'Nor me,' said another.

Dawlish remained by the window, oblivious even to the opening of the bedroom door, but the subject of the group's discussion appeared to be exhausted. The men went on to talk about farming and the fortunes farmers were supposed to be making.

'Hallo, darling,' said Felicity, 'getting a tip on fat stock prices?'

Dawlish swung round.

'Hallo, my sweet! No, I—' he stopped, abruptly. Why should he spoil dinner with talk of Dickerson. 'I was intrigued by the natives,' he dissembled.

'So was I,' said Felicity.

Dawlish looked at her searchingly.

'The bathroom's next door but one and I had a window open, too,' she went on. 'I wonder if that's all there is to it, Pat? Just an unpleasant fellow who thinks that a fat salary and good living conditions gives him the right to share a room when he feels like it?'

'Could be,' admitted Dawlish. 'On the other hand, Bill Trivett isn't a man to be troubled by trifles—and that certainly wouldn't give grounds for Yard intervention, even if an angry husband did make complaints. Remember, there's no trace of these women—I looked through Bill's report,' he added, 'which doesn't add much to what we already know. I wish I could believe that Bill's told us everything.'

Felicity shrugged her shoulders. 'Well, I expect we'll find out. I wonder how Sheila's getting on—I half expected her to ring through by now.'

Just before half-past seven they went downstairs; a table was reserved for them and dinner was excellent—there was even a half-bottle of Chablis, conjured up Dawlish knew not how. Nor did he care, for it was just the touch he wanted. They were preoccupied, but the preoccupation did not go very deep—although each time the door opened Felicity glanced towards it as if half-expecting to see Sheila.

She did not arrive until half past nine.

When she did, she surprised them—for she went to their room, without sending a message and, slipping inside, stood against the door with her back to it. She was pale and breathing heavily and both Dawlish and Felicity leaned towards her in consternation.

'What—' began Dawlish.

'Sheila!' exclaimed Felicity.

'I—I think I'm just being foolish,' said Sheila, between gasps. 'I had to walk down and—and I thought I was followed. I took what I thought was a short cut across a copse, and there were all manner of odd noises.' She laughed shakily.

'I think we'd better go down and have a drink,' said Dawlish, quietly. 'It'll steady you.'

'No, I'd rather not.' Colour was returning to Sheila's cheeks and she smiled more naturally. 'I think I've just been silly,' she repeated. 'I can't explain it—there's an atmosphere at the Grange which almost frightened me. But—' she drew a deep breath— '*he* couldn't have been nicer.'

Dawlish pulled a chair up for her.

'Tell us.'

'He couldn't have been nicer,' repeated Sheila, 'and yet I dislike him intensely. He—'

She described Dickerson so vividly that he might have been standing in the room with them. Dawlish, who knew Sheila fairly well, was surprised that the man had created so strong an impression on his level-headed cousin. The flight from the Grange was certainly out of keeping with everything he knew of her. That Dickerson could have brought about such a change in so short a time was disturbing.

'When I went to his study,' Sheila went on, 'he smiled at me—he's *always* smiling!' She paused, but the others did not interrupt. 'Well, he had another *Daily Mirror* on his desk, opened at the middle page, and asked me if I'd read it. Of course, I had to admit that I had. He laughed and told me that it was impossible for him to get local servants, although none had ever left his employ for any good reason. He said that he found country people quite incomprehensible, that he'd long given up trying to understand them, but that he hoped I would accept the position of fourth housekeeper. The three previous ones had left of their own free will, resigning without giving any reason, and he could hardly be held blameworthy for what happened afterwards.'

Sheila stopped and Dawlish murmured:

'A gentleman who believes in the direct approach!'

'He certainly does! The odd thing is, I half-believed him. Yet Maude—the maid—is scared stiff by him. She begged me not to stay even after I'd seen him. The other servants move about like mice and I haven't heard a voice raised. Even the taxi-driver was subdued. There *must* be something.'

Dawlish smiled, reflectively.

'It's a curious business, but'—he beamed at her—'I shouldn't worry any more about it, Sheila. Since you've left and turned him down—'

'Turned him down?' Sheila's eyebrows rose. 'I haven't done anything of the kind. I've accepted the job.'

Felicity exclaimed: 'After all that?'

'Why, yes,' said Sheila, 'I just can't see any practical reason why I shouldn't. It's all a matter of impressions, and there must be an explanation. With you two close at hand I shall feel safe enough—' she spoke, perhaps, a little too emphatically.

Dawlish's smile was worried.

'Do you think we ought to let her go back, Fel?'

'There isn't any question of "letting" me,' said Sheila, warmly, 'I'm going. I can't understand why it affected me so much. I—I told him that I would think it over and ring him up later in the evening. I left my case there. He wanted to send me down in a taxi but there wasn't one available, that's why I had to walk. It's not too far, although going back won't be so good, it's nearly all uphill.'

'And dark,' murmured Dawlish.

'Ye-es. There was a moon earlier, but it'll be set by now.'

In spite of her determination, Dawlish knew that she was torn two ways. Something had frightened her, though she did not like admitting it. He imagined that she had kept her poise in front of Dickerson and only the imagined—or *had* it been real?—follower through the trees had affected her. Now, in the safety of the well-lit room, that angered her.

He wondered whether he would be justified in allowing her to go back; she might say that there was no question of 'letting', but if he took a strong enough line she would give the whole thing up. Against that, the mystery was intriguing and there was an even more significant factor—Trivett's interest in it.

'Do you know the road well enough to go back?' he asked.

'Oh, yes, it's simple enough to follow.' Sheila had quite regained her composure and it was easy to see that she was regretting her earlier lack of control.

Dawlish said abruptly: 'Why shouldn't we give you a lift? Passing motorists are obliging that way. I'll take the car out and I'll start off in'—he glanced at his watch—'five minutes precisely. I'll pick you up outside, Fel, if you're game, and we'll collect Sheila at the corner.'

Before either of them could comment he had left the room.

'Fel, I *am* sorry. I didn't think he'd—'

Felicity laughed. 'It's never any use trying to imagine what he'll do.'

'Will he try to see Dickerson, do you think?'

'It wouldn't surprise me,' said Felicity, 'nor would I be surprised if we end up at the Grange for the night, he's quite capable of faking a break-down! It wouldn't be a bad idea to put a few things in a bag.' She hurried about the room, flinging the necessaries for the night into the smaller suitcase and, five minutes after Dawlish had left, they went downstairs—Sheila, as planned, walking on ahead.

The moon was down.

Footsteps echoed clearly, and not far away she heard the deep-powered note of a car. At the corner of the road Sheila paused and looked over her shoulder, then stopped and, as the M.G. drew near, held up her hand.

Dawlish applied the brakes, opened a window and asked loudly whether she wanted a lift. She replied that she did. Two people passed during the exchange, still within earshot as Dawlish said in the kindly voice of one extending a favour:

'Oh, *that's* all? Yes, I'll take you gladly. You don't mind the back?'

'Not at all.'

Once Sheila was in, Dawlish started off again. The light from the masked headlamps was enough for him to pick out the corner where the taxi had turned and he swung round it. As he changed gear again, he called:

'If there has to be any talking, leave it to me.'

He turned into the drive, pulling up with the nose of the

M.G. pointing towards the door, so that the lights would shine on anyone who came out.

The door opened abruptly; a faint light shone through, and someone said:

'You damned fool!'

CHAPTER SEVEN

THE HOSPITABLE MR. DICKERSON

Dawlish heard the words distinctly, although they were uttered in a low-pitched angry voice. They broke off abruptly.

Dickerson was standing on the porch, only a yard or so in front of the M.G., the lights of which shone on his legs and up as far as his chest.

'Hallo, hallo!' hailed Dawlish. 'Anyone about—oh, hal-*lo*!' He appeared to see Dickerson for the first time. 'Here she is, all safe and sound! Miss—er—'

'What does this mean?' demanded Dickerson. There was no hidden note of laughter now, only apprehension. Dawlish knew that the other had wrongly identified the arrivals. He recovered his poise quickly.

Dawlish grinned with the jolly assurance of one who had just done a good turn to a stranger. 'Just given a friend of yours a lift. Nasty hill to walk up in the dark!' He beamed widely as Sheila climbed out of the car.

'Miss Lynd!' exclaimed Dickerson; there was no doubt of the relief in his voice. 'I *am* sorry you tried to walk back, I expected you to come by taxi. This is very good of you, sir, very good indeed,' he added to Dawlish.

41

'Not a bit,' rumbled the large man. 'In fact a selfish motive! Short of water, more hills about here than I thought. Could you oblige?'

'Of course. I'll send a maid—'

'Terribly sorry to be such a nuisance,' said Dawlish. 'Not having the best of times, as a matter of fact. My wife—nasty headache.' He paused, awkwardly. '*Dare* I trouble you for an aspirin?'

'Your wife?' echoed Dickerson, blankly.

'Oh, yes, of course—Fel, we've found a good Samaritan, good thing we nearly knocked Miss'—he paused—'did you say Lynd?'

'Yes,' said Sheila, very quickly.

'Splendid! Glad to know you, Miss Lynd!' He lowered his voice. 'Help my wife out, will you—she suffers from megrim—hits her suddenly,' he added for Dickerson's benefit. 'She can hardly move. A breath of fresh air will do her the world of good. Next to a cup of tea, I can't think of anything that would be better!'

Felicity, getting out of the car, uttered a realistic groan. Dickerson, standing undecided, drew a deep breath and spoke with a heartiness which was obviously forced.

'Perhaps she would like to rest here for a little while, sir. We can get her some tea.'

'Oh, *no!*' exclaimed Dawlish. 'Shouldn't dream of putting you to so much trouble.' Felicity groaned again. 'Oh, my pet, is it as bad as that? Well I suppose—if you *insist*, Mr.—'

Dickerson spoke quickly.

'Please follow me.' To Sheila he said: 'Miss Lynd, I wonder if you would go to the kitchen and ask Maude to make some tea and bring some aspirins?' He pushed the door wider open and Dawlish helped Felicity in; she had ruffled her hair, and looked ready to faint, her lips twisted as if in pain.

Dickerson looked at her.

'Surely, your wife is ill, sir?'

'Ill?' echoed Dawlish. 'Oh, no, just a passing thing. She'll be all right? Won't you, pet?' He led Felicity to a chair. 'I say, what a jolly place you have here!'

Dickerson raised his eyebrows.

'It is pleasant, yes,' he conceded distantly.

'I'll bet it is!' exclaimed Dawlish, taking out a cigarette case. 'You don't know how much I appreciate your kindness, sir. Of course, it's my fault, my fault entirely.' He dropped his voice. 'Important job on hand—mustn't lose time. Government—hence the car.'

'Indeed,' said Dickerson. He looked at Felicity, who was resting her head against the back of the chair, her eyes closed. 'Are you sure that your wife doesn't need a doctor?'

'*Doctor?*' Dawlish shook his head. 'Right as a trivet in no time!'

Maude came in with a tea tray, and while Sheila busied herself pouring out, Dawlish continued a rather one-sided conversation of irrelevancies ending up with a request to know how far it was to Terne.

'You've just come from there,' said Dickerson.

'*What?*' gasped Dawlish. 'No! I didn't think that was anything more than a village! What an ass! And I've a room booked at the *George*. Strictly business!' he added, as if afraid that Dickerson would imagine he was misusing petrol. '*What* a night!'

He turned to fuss over Felicity, whispering through her hair: '*Get worse, Fel!*'

He straightened up, refusing a cup of tea with a fervour that Dickerson could only take it as a hint.

'Perhaps you'll have a drink?' he suggested, after a short pause.

'I say!' exclaimed Dawlish. '*Very* decent of you. To tell you the truth, I'm parched!'

'Whisky and soda?'

'*Is* there beer?'

'Oh, yes,' Dickerson turned and poured, while Dawlish babbled on.

'Between you and me, y'know'—He ran a finger round the inside of his collar—'we were married this morning, Mr—'

Looking startled, Dickerson gave his name.

'Do I understand that—' he stopped and smiled with a certain geniality.

Dawlish thought that for the first time Dickerson was convinced that this visitation was accidental. It was the impression he wanted to create, but he had to stifle more than a twinge of conscience at this capitalising on his honeymoon.

He smiled, as if with embarrassment.

'Thought we'd struck lucky, too—I had this little trip to make, secret business—did I tell you?—and it seemed an absolutely wizard idea to bring her along with me. I mean—well, you know!' He raised his tankard: 'Here's how!' He drank, deeply. 'Ah, that's just the tummy-tickler I wanted! Of course, I knew my wife had these headaches—strain and overwork y'know. She's been discharged from the A.T.S., as unfit, poor kid—I thought this holiday would buck her up. Still, there it is. I've booked at the *George* for the better part of a week—'

'So your headquarters will be in Terne?' asked Dickerson.

'Oh, rather! Charming spot, I hear.'

'I really don't think Mrs. Dawes should travel any further tonight,' Sheila said. 'She seems tired out—the slightest movement goes through her.'

'What?' gaped Dawlish. 'But we've booked our room! I was telling your—er—'

'It isn't far enough to harm her, surely,' said Dickerson quickly.

'If I had my way, I would put her to bed immediately and send for the doctor,' said Sheila, eyeing Dickerson steadily. 'Of course, you can let her go on, but, personally, I think it would be dangerous.'

Dawlish looked blankly at Dickerson.

'I say!' he said, 'she can't be as bad as all that!'

'I can only advise you,' said Sheila, coldly.

Dickerson said: 'Are you sure, Miss Lynd?'

'Quite sure.'

Dawlish caught her eye, but she gave no sign that she realised that he was trying to warn her not to go too far. He imagined that the conversational undertones he had heard from the lounge-hall had been a plot, hatched between her and Felicity to make sure that they were allowed to stay the night.

Then he caught Dickerson's gaze on him.

A few moments before he had thought that the owner of Wood Grange had been suspicious but that his suspicions had been dissipated; now, they were back at full strength. There was a calculating glint in Dickerson's eye, as if he suspected— even felt sure—that this visitation was deliberate. He also gave Dawlish the impression that he knew *why* such an effort was being made.

'This is a great pity, a *great* pity,' he said, and for the first time that night the echo of a laugh was in his voice. 'Of course, I will take your advice, Miss Lynd!' Before Dawlish could stop him he was at the telephone. He gave a number, still talking to Sheila. 'Will you and one of the maids take Mrs.—Dawes, was the name?—' Dawlish nodded, 'to the spare room, Maude will know which one. I will get a doctor here at once.'

Dawlish gulped.

'No, really old man—I can't—all this trouble—'

'It's no trouble at all,' Dickerson assured him, heartily. 'There is a good friend of mine who lives near, and he will come gladly. A doctor, although no longer practising,' he added.

'Er—remarkably good of him,' murmured Dawlish. '*Remarkably* good. But—'

'Hallo,' said Dickerson into the telephone—'is that Dr. Brett's residence . . . yes, I'll hold on.' He smiled at Dawlish, who took refuge behind his tankard, until Dickerson spoke again. 'Brett? . . . Hallo, doctor! I'm sorry to call you so late, but I wonder if you would be good enough to come here . . . A lady who—er. Yes, will you? . . . Thanks!' He replaced the receiver and smiled at Dawlish. '*That* was soon settled,' he said, 'I'm sure that Dr. Brett won't upset your wife, he's an admirable fellow.'

'Too kind,' mumbled Dawlish. 'I feel very guilty—troubling you like this.'

'It's no trouble at all,' Dickerson assured him blandly.

'No,' thought Dawlish. It was a delight, in fact.

He was quite convinced that Dickerson suspected Felicity of malingering, that he had sent for the doctor because he wanted to make sure. Dawlish saw the smile in his eyes and understood why so many people disliked him. It would be nonsensical to suggest that Dickerson had a frightening effect; it was more that he appeared to have a card up his sleeve, ready to play at the crucial moment. No fool, and a hard man to outwit.

Did he suspect Sheila?

'It's time I stopped rambling!' Dawlish said sharply to himself. 'I'm not in good form.' He turned to Dickerson with a simulated concern. 'I don't mind admitting that I feel very bad about this. *Very* bad. Look here!' He brightened up, as if inspired. 'If you'll be good enough to put Felicity up for the night, I'll go back to Terne! How about that!' His words trailed off under Dickerson's steady gaze.

'I shouldn't dream of separating man and wife,' said Dickerson, blandly, 'I insist that you stay here for the night, Mr. Dawes, and you must not think that you are giving me any trouble. I'm sure you will be relieved when the doctor has been and made his diagnosis.'

'Er—oh, rather,' said Dawlish. 'If he doesn't make her worse. She's very nervy you know.' He gave a hollow laugh. 'I think you ought to prepare Dr.—what was the name?'

'Brett.'

'Dr. Brett, for an unusual case,' Dawlish continued, in a sombre voice.

'I will,' Dickerson assured him, gently.

Sounds from the hall suggested that Felicity was being helped up the stairs.

'You know, I ought to go and lend a hand,' Dawlish said. 'Not fair, after all, to—'

'I assure you that your wife is receiving excellent attention,' said Dickerson.

'Oh, I know! But all the same—' Dawlish took another pull at his beer, put the tankard down and moved very quickly to the door before Dickerson had time to stop him.

Felicity and Sheila, with Maude just behind them, were disappearing at the head of the stairs. He hurried after them. When he looked back, he saw Dickerson staring at him with a thoughtful expression on his handsome face.

He reached the room that had been allocated to Felicity.

'Er—how's everyone?' he asked brightly, gazing at the little group while adding in a loud stage-whisper: 'Miss Lynd, don't let her know—*doctor.*' He mouthed the word '*Doctor,*' once again, turned and almost bumped into Dickerson. 'Why, hallo,' he said. 'I was just warning Miss Lynd not to—well, you know what!'

'I know,' said Dickerson, significantly.

Felicity gave a realistic groan.

'She'll never be able to keep it up,' thought Dawlish, but he was beginning to enjoy himself. It was exhilarating to create a situation and then see how it worked out. He turned away, taking out his cigarette-case. Dickerson produced a lighter.

'Thanks,' he said. 'Mr. er—er—'

'Dickerson,' said the other.

'Oh, I'm sorry! Names are difficult to get, first time, aren't they? What a day! You a married man?' he inquired, shooting a sidelong glance.

'I am a widower,' said Dickerson, stiffly.

'Oh, I say! Bad luck! Still that's life, you know. I wonder if I may telephone the *George* to tell them that I won't be along tonight? Hotels are so difficult these days and if I don't turn up they might decide to let someone else have the room tomorrow. I'd hate to impose on you any longer than a night!' He laughed.

'I don't think you need fear that,' said Dickerson, 'but telephone by all means.'

'I am beginning to dislike you intensely,' thought Dawlish.

He was led to the study, where Dickerson waved him to a telephone.

'Don't bother about the number. Just ask for the *George*,' said Dickerson. 'The exchange will put you through.'

'Oh, good idea!' exclaimed Dawlish; but there was no response from the exchange. He rattled the telephone up and down, grumbling, but the only sound had a hollow note. Dickerson hardly tried to hide his smile as Dawlish said: '*Aren't* they a long time?'

He knew, however, that the line was dead and that Dickerson was aware of it.

CHAPTER EIGHT

THE DUBIOUS DOCTOR

'But it was perfectly all right when I telephoned Dr. Brett,' said Dickerson, as if the failure of the telephone astonished him. 'What a remarkable thing!'

He shrugged his shoulders.

'I'm afraid we shall have to wait until the morning before we get it put right, Mr. Dawes, but Dr. Brett will telephone a message for you, I'm sure.'

'Ah, good idea!' said Dawlish, more brightly.

He had little doubt that the man had expected him to ask for the telephone and that the line had been disconnected inside the house. It was unlikely that it was cut. The smoothness of the disconnection suggested that there was a switch in the house which could be used for just such a purpose—and, if there were, it meant that Dickerson was accustomed to preventing visitors from telephoning.

It was half-past ten when a maid tapped on the door and announced Dr. Brett.

'Come in, doctor, come in!' said Dickerson, warmly.

Into the room stepped a short, bearded man, carrying a bag.

His eyes were bright and his manner nervous as he viewed Dawlish.

'But my dear Dickerson, I thought you said—a *lady*!'

The man's obvious astonishment impressed Dawlish unfavourably. It seemed to imply that Dickerson *should* have meant a woman. It was a fleeting thought, just as a quick exchange of glances between Dickerson and the stocky doctor was fleeting. Smoothly Dickerson explained what had happened, and before Dawlish could join them they were both walking towards Felicity's room. The door of the study closed with a decided snap.

'Well, well!' murmured Dawlish.

He went swiftly to the door, and held his ear to it. Brett appeared to be protesting and Dickerson insisting on some point which Dawlish wished he knew about. Reluctantly he returned to the desk and sat on the corner, swinging his legs idly. He was like that when Dickerson returned.

Dawlish jumped down.

'How is she?' he demanded, quickly.

'Come, give the doctor time!' exhorted Dickerson. 'I feel sure that he will be able to help her,' he added, 'he is a very clever practitioner.'

Had Sheila not been in the room with Felicity, Dawlish would have insisted on being present; as it was, he thought that any insistence would be suspected. He waited, as if on tenterhooks, inwardly hoping that Felicity would be able to hoodwink the doctor for the time being, at all events.

Then he heard footsteps and Sheila's voice; two people were walking across the hall, but the other did not sound like Dr. Brett.

Sheila was saying: 'Does Dr. Brett always like to see his patients by themselves, Maude?'

'Well'm,' began Maude, 'I dunno.'

Dawlish pursed his lips. Sheila could not have said more clearly that Brett was alone with Felicity and Dawlish did not propose to allow Felicity to be at the mercy of any doctor, real or false, good-intentioned or bad. Nor did he propose to waste time in arguing with Dickerson; if the man were suspicious, so be it. Without a 'by-your-leave', Dawlish stepped to the door.

'Where are you going?' demanded Dickerson, sharply.

'Oh, come!' said Dawlish. 'The doctor's finished, didn't you hear Miss—*what's* her name?—say so?' He sped along to Felicity's room, turned the handle and stepped in.

She was in bed, screened by Brett, who was leaning over her: in his hand was a hypodermic syringe.

'Hallo, hallo!' said Dawlish, striding forward. 'Everything in order, eh?' He did not need telling that the expression in Felicity's eyes was one of relief; he guessed that she had been on the point of crying out, but had left it to the last minute. Brett turned, his eyes glittering dangerously.

'What does this interruption mean, sir?'

'Interruption?' asked Dawlish, his voice still jolly but bemused. 'That's all right, I'm her husband. What's the report, doctor? She doesn't *look* too well.' He had a sharp fear that she had already received an injection and a fierce anger flared up within him.

'Your wife is suffering from hysteria,' said Brett repressively. 'She must have rest and I am administering a sedative.' He gripped Felicity's wrist and moved the syringe.

Dawlish reached his side in three strides and literally shouldered him away. The syringe dropped to the carpet.

'What the devil are you doing?' cried Dickerson, who had followed him closely.

'Doing!' gasped Dawlish, pointing a quivering finger at Brett. 'He was going to *inject* something! She's allergic to them—always has been—might have killed her!' He gazed at Brett as he would at a toad. The nervous little doctor's hands were trembling, he bit his lip and then, as if to try to preserve some remnants of self-possession, stooped down to retrieve the syringe.

'Mr. Dawes,' said Dickerson, evenly, 'I have to remind you that at considerable inconvenience I have given your wife shelter, sent for medical attention, and put a room at your disposal for the night. The least you can do, in return, is to allow the doctor to prescribe and administer treatment. You have yourself admitted how badly your wife has been suffering, and Dr. Brett has diagnosed hysteria. Perhaps you are not aware of the seriousness of such an affliction?'

'Affliction?' echoed Dawlish. 'Er—look here, I'm terribly sorry, but there are limits, you know. No injections. I'm frightfully sorry about barging into you, doctor,' he added to the little man, who was now staring at him with unveiled malignance, 'but you're a bit quick off the mark, aren't you?'

'Do you or do you not wish your wife to receive treatment?' demanded Dickerson in an angry voice.

'Oh, treatment, but not—'

Dawlish stopped, knowing that Dickerson was no longer listening to him. In fact Dickerson was looking across at Dr. Brett. Some communication passed between them.

'I say—' began Dawlish, but stopped short, for Dickerson had put his right hand to his pocket. It might have been a casual movement but he might carry a gun.

'Mr. Dawes,' said Dickerson, very softly, 'I think it is time you gave me an explanation of your visit here. I understand from Dr. Brett that there is nothing at all the matter with your wife. *Nothing at all the matter,*' he repeated, and Dawlish thought that something poked against the inside of his pocket. 'Just *why* did you come here, Mr. Dawes? Tell me that.'

CHAPTER NINE

GLOVES OFF

Dawlish glared at Brett as if he were in the grip of an overpowering rage.

'Nothing the matter with her?' echoed Dawlish in a tense voice, 'and you ask *me* for an explanation. Why did he want to inject something in her, then? Answer me that?'

He made a movement towards Dickerson, who took his hand from his pocket. All doubts were settled, for he held a snub-nosed automatic. Dawlish saw it, stopped and gaped. Felicity did not move.

'Isn't it time you stopped acting?' asked Dickerson, smoothly, 'and not very convincingly at that. You see that I have a gun, Mr. Dawes. Don't misunderstand me. I find it necessary to protect myself against criminal individuals—or *thieves*,' he added. 'You have forced yourself into my house on a foolish pretext. You ask why Dr. Brett was going to give your wife an injection. The answer is perfectly simple—he was doing nothing of the kind. He pretended to—we arranged this little drama in order to force you into an admission, such as you have made.'

'I've made no admission,' denied Dawlish, sharply.

'You were far too anxious to prevent our harmless little experiment,' said Dickerson, 'and in any case Dr. Brett has told me that there is nothing at all the matter with your wife. You really can't keep it up any longer, Mr. Dawes. You have acted the part of a nincompoop more than adequately—the character sits well on you—but I have not been deceived. Why did you force your way into my house?'

Dawlish said: 'Am I wrong, or did you invite me in?'

'You invited yourself and you know it!' snapped Dickerson, moving the gun forward. 'Answer me!'

'We-ell,' said Dawlish, 'if you insist.' He turned and looked at Felicity, his face wooden, his mind seeking a plausible explanation strong enough to convince Dickerson without giving the whole game away. Dickerson's prompt self-justification for having a gun suggested that he was not prepared to take undue risks, and so far he had a case for using it. Even if there were trouble and someone got hurt, he would still have a case, for Brett's evidence would be reasonably conclusive proof that the 'Dawes's' had gate-crashed.

'Well?' Dickerson's voice held a dangerous note.

Dawlish said, briskly: 'Right. Well, we'll play it your way. Take a long look at my wife, will you?'

In the pause that followed, Dawlish spoke again.

'You're not so quick as I thought you'd be, Dickerson. Most people say that she is very much like her sister.'

'What has her sister to do with me?' demanded Dickerson, a little uneasily.

'Not so very long ago,' said Dawlish, 'you applied for a resident housekeeper. My wife's sister—Felicity wasn't my wife then, but that doesn't matter—applied for the job and got it. She disappeared. Her name was Hilda Bryant. Her husband came home on leave and tried to get in touch with her, but failed. I understand that you put him off with many specious excuses. There was little he could do, as he was on embarkation leave, but he *did* talk to me.'

Dickerson took a short step forward, staring intently at Felicity; Brett looked as if he had received a shock. Obviously Dawlish had struck them on a raw spot. They exchanged quick glances and the dubious doctor licked his lips, then turned and began to put oddments back in his case.

Dickerson put the gun into his pocket but kept his hand about it.

'Why the devil didn't you say so at once?' he demanded.

'Because I didn't think I'd get a straight answer,' said Dawlish. 'Felicity and I had decided that *she* would apply for the job, but'—he shrugged—'we made one or two inquiries and found that you were already fixed up.'

'Who told you that?' rasped Dickerson.

'It's common knowledge in Terne,' said Dawlish, 'I heard it from some of the staff of the *George*. As a matter of fact the barman told me that the "new one" was in the bar. I took my car out, waited half-way up the road, and offered her a lift. Very simple, you see.'

'Ye-es,' admitted Dickerson, 'you're not the fool you look, Dawes.'

'Oh, come!' protested Dawlish, as if embarrassed.

'And yet in some ways you are,' said Dickerson. 'If you had come to see me, I could have given you every assurance that I knew nothing about what happened to your sister-in-law.' His words were virtuous, but spoken rather too quickly. 'Am *I* to blame if a lot of old women start a scurrilous rumour which the papers take up? The police have been here several times, but have been compelled to admit that I am in no way responsible for the behaviour of servants who leave my employ.'

'Oh,' said Dawlish. 'Haven't the police seen your weak spot, yet?'

Dickerson stiffened. 'I don't like that remark, Dawes!'

'There is going to be a great deal more you don't like,' promised Dawlish, gently. 'Quick work with the telephone—or wasn't it? A cock-and-bull story about the little doctor and the imaginary injection—wasn't he going to put Felicity to sleep and give you grounds for using a strong hand with me? Or wasn't he?' He grinned. 'Catch,' he said, and tossed his cigarette case across the room.

Dickerson dodged to one side—and Dawlish strode forward, gripped his right arm and jerked it from his pocket; the gun dropped but Dawlish caught it before it reached the floor, slipped it into his pocket and stood back, as if nothing had happened.

'Thanks,' said Dawlish, 'that's much better.' He regarded Dickerson with his head on one side, then turned to Brett. 'Doctor,' he said, 'have you a suitable injection which will help to steady your friend after such a severe shock?'

Dickerson drew a deep breath but managed to control his features. The quick turning of the tables had obviously taken him completely by surprise. He looked from Dawlish to Felicity, then on to Brett.

'You don't understand,' Dickerson said, at last. 'I have a great number of valuables in this house, Dawes. I have to protect myself. As a matter of fact'—he paused, and Dawlish could almost see his mind working—'two of the housekeepers were dismissed because they grew too curious about my safe. One of them actually stole a bundle of notes from my desk! No wonder they're not anxious to advertise their whereabouts!'

Slowly, sadly, Dawlish shook his head.

'I don't believe you,' he said.

'It's true!' snapped Dickerson. 'I have to be very careful whom I employ. How do you think I obtained a licence for—for my gun, if the police did not recognise that I had good reason to be afraid of thieves? Supposing I do make sure that no one can use the telephone if they force their way in here? Surely that is mere common-sense.'

Dawlish widened his eyes.

'Is is a habit?' he drawled.

'It's happened before!'

'Indeed? But a repetition of the same theme does not make me believe it. What happened to my wife's sister, Dickerson?'

'I tell you I don't know!'

'No?' murmured Dawlish. 'Does the doctor, I wonder?' He turned a speculative eye on Brett, who was edging towards the door. 'Would he have used that syringe of which he's so fond? I mean, could it be conspiracy? He came *expecting* to use the syringe, didn't he? How startled and sadly disappointed he was to be confronted with a man and not a woman.'

'Don't talk nonsense!' gasped Brett, shrilly.

'Now listen to me, Dawes,' said Dickerson in a reasoning voice, 'you're allowing your imagination to play tricks. Just because you came here thinking that I am some kind of monster—a modern Bluebeard!' he smiled, but it was a sickly effort—'you have over-dramatised everything. I'll make you a friendly offer. We've both got wrong ideas about each other, but that can be put right. Stay here for the night, and, first thing in the morning, go to see the Superintendent of Police in Terne. Ask him if I haven't told you the truth. *I'm* not worried, but we can't allow these doubts and suspicions to get worse.'

'No—o,' murmured Dawlish, after some reflection. 'No, perhaps not.' His face cleared and he said decisively: 'All right, Dickerson, I'll take you. No one can ever say that I wouldn't play ball! But don't let your friend the doctor get too busy with his syringe, will you? In fact—' he stepped swiftly towards the doctor's bag, lifted it and dropped it on the bed, near Felicity's arm. 'Investigate, sweet,' he said. 'We'll take the syringe and all there is in it to the policeman. If it *is* a harmless sedative—well, what could be fairer than that?'

'You've no right—' began Brett.

'Now, doctor!' Dickerson was almost genial. 'There is no reason why Mr. Dawes should not continue to behave foolishly a little longer if he thinks it will help him. Let him have the syringe, we have no reason to fear the result of the analysis of the drug, have we? Have we?' he insisted, as Brett gulped.

'N—n—no!' muttered the doctor.

'Excellent, excellent!' exclaimed Dickerson. 'Keep the syringe, Dawes—true, you have obtained it in a somewhat unorthodox manner, but you are not an orthodox man, are you? I am beginning to like you—believe me!' He laughed, gaily. 'Let us leave them, doctor! Mr. Dawes tells me that they were married only this morning and I feel sure that they do not want company *all* night. Is there anything else you would like, Mr. Dawes? Coffee? Sandwiches?' He was shepherding Brett to the door and Dawlish felt that it would be folly to go further than he had done.

Felicity had the syringe.

Dickerson turned to her. Now that he was more composed, he became again the handsome man with the polished manner. He was almost gay. 'I do congratulate you on your acting Mrs. Dawes. Quite professional. But I must not detain you. I will have some coffee sent up.' He bowed and smiled again.

The door safely shut on the two men, Felicity began to laugh. Dawlish eyed her for some seconds, his smile widening. At length he began to chuckle.

Twenty minutes later, there was a discreet tap at the door, and Sheila appeared, carrying coffee and sandwiches.

She spoke quickly in a nervous undertone. 'Pat, I don't think Dickerson is convinced that I've nothing to do with you, I think he sent one of the maids to watch me. Tell me quickly what has happened.'

Dawlish gave her a brief resume of what had occurred.

'Isn't there any sugar?' asked Felicity, a little sleepily.

'They've run out,' said Sheila briefly, 'but there's saccharin in the coffee-pot. Dickerson—' she stopped, seeing a startling change in Dawlish's expression. 'Pat, why are you looking at me like that?'

'Not at you,' murmured Dawlish, 'through you, to the ingenuous but very persistent Mr. Dickerson! So there are saccharin tablets in the coffee? I suppose he took them from his private supply.'

'He certainly took them out of a bottle,' admitted Sheila, 'but I don't see—' she broke off abruptly.

'Ah,' said Dawlish, 'but you see it now, don't you? Saccharin indeed!' He smiled, cheerfully. 'Alas, no coffee for us. I think they're worried because I collared the syringe and are anxious not to let the police examine it. Sheila, be very careful. Notice anything the least bit out of the ordinary and yell for us if you think there's trouble.'

'Right,' said Sheila, quietly: 'Thank God, my room is next to yours.'

Dawlish did not lock the door behind her, but lifting the coffee pot poured its contents down the hand-basin in the bathroom. When he returned Felicity was eating a sandwich.

'I hope that's all right,' said Dawlish, a little lugubriously.

'I'm too hungry to care,' said Felicity, taking another bite.

Five minutes later Dawlish switched off the light.

* * *

There was a sound, brief, inconclusive, and Dawlish was awake in an instant. It could have come from the door or the window. He thought the door more likely, for Dickerson would expect him to be in a drugged sleep.

A faint, a very faint light permeated the room, and by it Dawlish made out the figure of Dickerson. Dawlish closed his eyes as a thin pencil of light shone first on his face and then, after a pause, on the table. An infinitesimal clink followed, as of the syringe being lifted. Dawlish knew that Dickerson was standing still, afraid that one or the other of them would wake up. Not for several seconds did he turn away and stealthily return to the doorway. Dawlish allowed him to reach the door before turning over and uttering a vast sigh. He grinned to himself as he put his hand beneath his pillow, closing it over an aspirin bottle, into which he had poured the contents of the syringe, itself now filled with water.

Felicity stirred and then stiffened, before saying in a small voice:

'Pat! Pat, are you there?'

'Yes, of course,' said Dawlish.

'Oh!' She sounded relieved. 'I thought I heard something.'

'Sheer fancy,' Dawlish assured her, 'I expect you've been dreaming.'

Felicity murmured unintelligibly. Soon her even breathing told him that she had gone to sleep again. Dawlish pondered over the wisdom of leaving the room and trying to find out whether Dickerson and Brett were talking together, but decided that subtlety was the order for the night—and soon dozed off.

He would have had little reward had he followed Dickerson, beyond an amused satisfaction when the man went to the bathroom and carefully emptied out the syringe, washing all traces of the contents away. That done he went to his study and telephoned the doctor to say that all danger had been removed.

'You're sure?' asked Brett, sharply.

'I've just emptied and washed it,' said Dickerson, 'Dawlish isn't as smart as he thinks.'

'Dawlish? I thought his name was Dawes!'

'So did I, but there's a driving licence in his car,' said Dickerson, with a self-satisfied chuckle. 'Oh, he's no fool, but not quite as clever as he thinks he is.'

'Don't be too sure,' said Brett, slowly. 'I don't like his confidence. I think you should find out whether the Bryant woman really has a sister.'

After a pause, Dickerson said slowly:

'Ye—es, you're probably right. I'll check up—but there's no need to worry tonight.'

'Another thing I'd do, if I were you, would be to check up on this Lynd woman,' said Brett.

'Oh, *she's* all right!'

'Maybe, and maybe not,' said Brett sharply. 'Why don't you telephone Harris right away? He can make inquiries in London, both about Dawlish and the Lynd woman—you have her London address, haven't you? And Dawlish's, if you've seen the licence.'

'I think you're making too much fuss, but—oh, all right, I'll give Harris a ring.'

'I can't help feeling that I've seen Dawlish before,' Brett went on. 'I can't call him to mind, but—anyhow, you ask Harris.'

The dubious doctor rang off, and Dickerson immediately put a call through to one Leonard K. Harris, who slept in a room above a small suite of offices, on the doors of which was painted:

'*The Leonard Harris Inquiry Bureau*'. At first Harris sounded disgruntled, but as the voice went on, he began to smile.

It seemed that in the course of his business he had come to know the reputation of Patrick Dawlish rather well.

CHAPTER TEN

THE YOUNG MAN WITH THE MILK

Sheila woke up soon after six o'clock.

Unmistakably she had heard masculine footsteps cross the hall, then the voice of Dr. Brett, saying irritably:

'What *is* it, at *this* time of the morning.'

A door closed. Sheila wrapped her dressing-gown more tightly about her, and tip-toed along towards the study. She heard the key turn in the lock before Dickerson began to speak and caught only the first few words: then Dickerson's voice faded—presumably he had walked to his desk, which was by the window

The few words were enough, for Dickerson said:

'You were right, Brett, there's something behind it, Harris knows Dawlish. He's—'

Sheila tried to hear the next sentence and Brett's reply, but failed. She turned back along the passage, alarmed and intending to see Dawlish—but as she reached the door of her own room she heard the whine of a vacuum cleaner.

Suddenly servants seemed to be everywhere.

She dressed after a quick bath, giving herself no time to linger in the luxury of the blue bathroom.

Outside Dawlish's room one of the maids was busy dusting. Shrugging her shoulders Sheila went downstairs. Maude was in the hall; she looked up but hastily averted her eyes, as if to declare that she had done her best and, now that her advice had been ignored, the responsibility was wholly Sheila's.

A third maid was busy in the kitchen.

Sheila went out by the door leading from the kitchen passage.

She heard the sound of a horse and cart coming along a secondary drive which, Dickerson had told her on the previous afternoon, led to the back of the house and was used mainly by the tradesmen.

A piebald pony came in sight pulling a milk-float. In the float, with one hand holding the reins, stood a young man whistling, obviously at peace with the world.

He was a pleasant-looking young man, clad in an open-necked shirt, a well-cut jacket, and flannels. He did not see Sheila until he was almost on a level with her, then, with a startled jolt, the float came to a standstill. The young man regarded Sheila with a smile which held a hint of surprise and, perhaps, something deeper.

'Good morning!'

'Good morning.'

'Glorious morning, isn't it?' said the young man.

'Lovely,' said Sheila, gravely.

He hesitated for a moment, and then contributed:

'Er—yes, it certainly is. I—er—'

'You'll find someone in the kitchen,' said Sheila.

'Oh, yes! There's always someone about here,' said the young man, as if delighted at the conversational opening. 'I've been here as early as five o'clock and been told that I've kept them waiting! Er—staying at the Grange?'

It could have been an impertinent question, but the young

man with the milk was no ordinary milkman. In spite of his slight air of embarrassment he was self-possessed and his voice and manner made him seem out of place—had he been walking along Jermyn Street with Dawlish he would have fitted in better. That was not all; he gave her the impression that he was surprised and even alarmed to see her at the Grange, and because of it she answered deliberately:

'I have just taken up a position here.'

'Oh,' said the young man, frowning; it made him look severe and very young. 'Housekeeper?' He barked the word.

'Yes.'

'Take my tip,' said the young man with the milk, 'and get away faster than you've come! No business of mine, I know, but one good turn deserves another!'

'I wasn't aware that I'd—' began Sheila.

'The very sight of you at this hour in the morning is a good turn enough for any man!' declared the milkman, smiling engagingly. 'I thought I had seen a vision! Er—seriously—'

He stopped, for the kitchen door opened and the maid appeared in the doorway; Sheila felt sure that the woman had been watching from the window. The young man hesitated, looked at Sheila with one eyebrow raised, then went on in a low-pitched voice:

'Look here, I'm not dishing out gratuitous advice for no reason—I mean, if you feel like a helping hand—I'm at Grange Farm Cottage. The farm's a mile down the road,' he added, 'you can't miss it.' He clicked his tongue and the pony moved sedately towards the house.

She was still standing there on his return journey, but now he gave the impression that he did not want to be seen talking to her.

He passed and Sheila watched him out of sight.

Had she been a genuine applicant for the job, had she been full of the joys of a new post in glorious surroundings, the stranger would have given her a severe jolt. As it was, she assumed that he was speaking out of the goodness of his heart and relaying the warning which anyone around Terne would think necessary. Yet it worried her, for she had been disconcerted by the steady gaze from the young man's grey eyes.

Before she had left to go to Terne on the previous evening, Dickerson had told her that on the following morning they would discuss her duties. At the moment, she had none. She wished it were safe to seek out Pat and Felicity, but decided it would be too risky. She wondered whether it would be wiser to write a note, but decided against that too.

Suddenly anxious for their safety, she went upstairs and asked the maid whether the visitors were up. Then she heard Dawlish humming to himself above a great splashing of water. The maid said, 'Yes'm.' None of the servants seemed able to converse in anything but monosyllables.

Relieved, Sheila went to her own room, feeling disinclined to finish her unpacking. The situation was too fluid and she did not seriously think that she would be staying long. On the other hand, even if Dawlish were suspected of being more than he professed, much more would depend on her staying at the Grange.

There was a sudden tap at her door, and Dickerson appeared, suave, impeccably dressed, the perfect employer.

'Good morning, Miss Lynd! I was told that you had been out in the grounds already, and knew that I would not be disturbing you. I hope that you slept well.'

'Very well, thank you,' said Sheila, formally.

'Good. Have you, by any chance, seen Mrs. Dawlish this morning?'

'Mrs. Dawes?' asked Sheila, quickly.

'I understand that we misheard the name last night—it is Dawlish,' said Dickerson, smoothly. He was watching her closely and she realised that he was trying to trap her into some kind of admission. She had nearly given herself away, and would have done so, but for having heard that snatch of conversation. 'Have you seen her this morning?' Dickerson went on.

'No, I didn't think she was up,' said Sheila.

'I wasn't sure,' said Dickerson. 'Miss Lynd—you will be quite frank with me, won't you?'

'Of course.'

'Had you met Mr. and Mrs. Dawlish at the *George*?'

'I saw them there,' said Sheila, quickly. Her heart began to beat fast. 'Why, is it important, Mr. Dickerson?'

'You aren't, by any chance, old acquaintances?'

'I don't understand you,' said Sheila, coldly. 'I told you last night that they had stopped while I was walking back here, and offered me a lift. I accepted, and they insisted on bringing me right to the door.'

'Oh, to be sure!' exclaimed Dickerson. 'Don't misunderstand me. As a matter of fact, Miss Lynd'—he edged further into the room—'I have a number of very valuable things in this house. I wondered if you could assure me of the Dawlish's *bona fides*. I had the impression last night that they attempted to force their way in here and I was somewhat perturbed.'

'I don't think you had any need to be,' said Sheila, steadily. 'There's nothing missing, is there?'

'Oh, no, no!' Dickerson assured her, 'but in the circumstances it is necessary for any householder to be a bit careful. Well, I will see you after breakfast, as we arranged. Oh, I should tell you this. Dr. Brett has the freedom of the house and I am always at home to a Mr. Cartwright, should he call. You won't forget the name?'

Dickerson went out, smiling urbanely, making her feel that he had deliberately mislead her over some point or other.

The vague misgivings continued until breakfast time, when Dawlish and Felicity came down. Dickerson was also at breakfast and insisted that Sheila should join them at the table. He was very gay and hospitable, even to the point of wishing that his guests could stay longer. 'But I know,' he added, 'that you, Mr. Dawlish, have pressing business to consider.'

'Oh, I have,' said Dawlish. He tapped his pocket, drawing attention to the syringe.

Dickerson went on smoothly:

'When you have satisfied yourself, I shall look forward to seeing you again, Mr. Dawlish.'

'By Jove, so shall I!' exclaimed Dawlish. 'We'll have to get everything cleared up, won't we?' He noted, but paid no outward attention to the fact that he was being addressed as 'Dawlish' instead of 'Dawes'. He guessed the reason for the change and was thoughtful, knowing that the M.G. had been examined. It was still outside the front door, but had been turned so that he could drive straight down the main drive.

From Sheila's expression he judged that she was trying to get word to him, but Dickerson gave them no opportunity, following even to the door of the car, waving gaily as Dawlish eased off the brakes and started down the drive. It was steeper than he remembered; nor had he realised that the turning into the main road was so blind. To reach the gates he had to swerve round a sharp bend, the slope making the car go faster than he intended.

'Marvel that we managed it so well last night,' he said to Felicity. 'I—ha*llo*!'

The car shot forward for the foot brake refused to hold. He grabbed the handbrake, but it had no effect either. They were twenty yards from the gates, which were wide open. He heard the rumble of a heavy vehicle in the road and caught a glimpse of it through the trees. He realised that he had not heard it until that moment, it had either just started or had been coasting downhill.

Felicity gripped the side of the window.

Dawlish pulled the wheel round, letting the M.G. run, almost broadside-on, into the bank. It scraped noisily, swayed to one side, lurched forward—and then came to a standstill. They were jerked upwards, their heads striking the canvas hood. Then the lorry passed the gates, a big heavy vehicle going at some speed.

Dawlish sat still, looking at Felicity.

'Pat, was that—'

'Dirty work on the brakes during the night, yes, indeed,' said Dawlish. 'Not a shadow of doubt, and I don't think that lorry passed by accident.'

'I wonder *why* he did it,' said Felicity, slowly.

'Dissatisfied even with the second story we pitched,' Dawlish said, as if the incident were only trivial, 'so he decided that an accident would look very convincing and the driver of the lorry would have been an extra source of evidence. Doubtless he would have said that I was driving too fast. Five minutes or so's work on the brakes would probably put them right after the tragedy. Yes, very neatly arranged. I don't think Sheila ought to stay.'

'Nor do I,' said Felicity, quickly.

'So, we'll walk back, after I've had a look at the brakes,' said Dawlish.

A very short inspection, and he straightened up with a grunt. 'Just as I thought, we are dealing with a pretty cool customer.'

He finished tightening the brakes, and, satisfied, drove into the road, turned the car and drove back.

Felicity stayed in the car as Dawlish rang the bell.

There was no immediate answer, but eventually Dickerson himself opened the door. There was a pregnant moment of silence before Dawlish said with every appearance of amiability:

'It didn't work, Dickerson.'

'I *beg* your pardon?'

'The little trick with the brakes,' said Dawlish, pleasantly.

'What the devil are you talking about?' snapped Dickerson.

'Such innocence!' sighed Dawlish. 'However, we'll deal with that later. My wife and I have been discussing the position of the charming Miss Lynd,' he added, 'and in view of everything we feel that we should warn her that it might not be a healthy spot for her here. You won't mind us advising her, I'm sure.'

Dickerson snarled: 'Get off these premises!'

'Oh, no,' said Dawlish. 'The time has come when we have to be very frank, and I don't propose to allow any young woman, even if she is a stranger to me, to stay here any longer than she must. That is, for just as long as it will take her to pack her bag.'

Dickerson drew a deep breath, and said:

'She has gone for a walk.'

'Then call her back,' said Dawlish.

'I shall do nothing of the kind,' said Dickerson. 'And don't trouble to keep up the pretence any longer, Dawlish, for I *know* she's your cousin!'

CHAPTER ELEVEN

NO SIGN OF SHEILA

Dickerson must have seen the change in Dawlish's expression; nothing else could have accounted for the way the man blanched and stepped back into the hall. Yet Dawlish's face looked wooden, only his eyes showed the sudden flare of anger—as much at his own folly in allowing Sheila to stay as at Dickerson's words.

'You do, do you?' said Dawlish. He stepped forward, pushing the man aside unceremoniously, and raised his voice, 'Sheila! Sheila! Come down, will you?'

There was no answer.

'Where is she?' he demanded harshly.

Dickerson said, softly: 'Isn't it time we had a talk, *Major* Dawlish?'

After a brief silence, Dawlish murmured:

'So you know as much as that, do you?'

'Miss Lynd will come to no harm if you are sensible,' said Dickerson. 'That is what I want to talk about.' The man's hands were unsteady and his lips were quivering; he was trying hard to make it look as if he was in a strong position, but he was frightened, finding it difficult to be convincing.

'Where is she?' Dawlish repeated dispassionately.

'She has gone into the grounds, and—'

'You know, this just won't do,' said Dawlish. He appeared to tower over the other man, giving an impression of over-whelming strength that he would, if necessary, use. 'Bring her here at once, Dickerson.'

Dickerson cowered back.

'I tell you she's gone out—'

'I tell you that you're making one of your really big mistakes,' said Dawlish. 'You—'

'Nothing will happen to her!' Dickerson was breathing heavily, his fears deepening. '*I* can't get her back, but if you stay here or if you try to queer our pitch, I can't be responsible for what happens.'

Dawlish said, musingly: '*Our* pitch.' He deliberated. 'Yours and Brett's? With someone else, perhaps? Sheila has gone the way of all the others, of course, but this time the angry relatives are on the doorstep. Are you going to get her, at once?'

'I tell you that I can't!'

'Too bad,' murmured Dawlish, '*much* too bad.' He moved forward, and Dickerson tried to back away, but Dawlish gripped the lapels of his coat and held him tightly. 'All right, if you want it that way. An eye for an eye, a tooth for a tooth, a body for a body. You can consider yourself my prisoner.'

'W-w-what are y-you t-talking about?' stammered Dickerson.

'It's really quite simple. If Sheila is a hostage, so are you. You're coming with me.'

'You—you can't—'

'Now, come,' chided Dawlish, 'you can't have it all your own way. You drive, Fel, and I'll get in the back with our Mr. Dickerson. Go up the hill and take the first side-road you see. There are many quiet copses about and I think Dickerson will yield to persuasion.'

'You can't do this!' shouted Dickerson. 'The servants will—will tell the police, I'll—'

'Perhaps they will,' said Dawlish, 'and perhaps they won't for there might be one or two little things they wouldn't like the police-to hear about.' He changed his hold, gripping the man's arm, forcing him towards the M.G. Felicity was already at the wheel and the engine was ticking over.

No one appeared, not even Maude.

As if all hope had been abandoned Dickerson allowed himself to be propelled into the car.

Cautiously, Felicity drove down the drive. She reached the corner without mishap, turned right and went up the hill. About half a mile farther on there was a narrow turning. Here Felicity stopped. 'Will this do?'

'Anywhere,' said Dawlish amiably, 'where I can have a quiet talk with Dickerson.'

Dickerson, trying to collect himself, managed to speak without stammering.

'This is an outrageous thing, Dawlish, I shall report it to the police as soon as I get back!'

Dawlish smiled at him. 'What gives you the idea that you're going to get back?' he inquired. 'Your other housekeepers haven't and I nearly had an accident myself. Why shouldn't you? Accidents,' he mused, 'are so conveniently arranged on hilly ground. A fall over a cliff, for instance. You don't remember where Sheila is, do you?'

Dickerson relapsed into sullen silence.

Felicity, turning into the side-road, said quietly:

'Ought we to have searched the house, Pat?'

'I don't think so,' said Dawlish. 'Dickerson might have more booby traps there and reinforcements might have been rushed up. Whatever roguery there is, he's not alone in it.'

'You—you're talking nonsense!' snapped Dickerson.

'Surely nonsense wouldn't enrage you to such a point?' said Dawlish, genially. 'It does not seem to have stopped you making some pretty extensive inquiries about me, the answers to which have obviously troubled you enough to attempt my life.'

'The police—' muttered Dickerson, only to stop too thoroughly frightened to go on.

Felicity drove past a thicket of hawthorn and on to a track leading through a copse. Dickerson looked about him furtively.

It was as well, reflected Dawlish somewhat ironically, that Dickerson had made inquiries and learned a little about him; his reputation was certainly much more horrific than his record.

'This will do nicely,' he said at last.

Felicity had stopped because it was impossible to go farther, in a shadowy clearing in the middle of the copse. The ground was damp underfoot and Dawlish, with a thought to the wheels of the M.G., hoped that it would not be too difficult to get it going again.

'Out with you,' he said sharply.

Once on the coarse, branch-strewn grass, Dickerson looked from one to the other. He started to speak, then changed his mind. There was no mistaking the fact that he was very frightened.

Dawlish put his head on one side, and asked aloud:

'How shall we start, I wonder?'

'*You* shouldn't need telling,' said Felicity, with just the right emphasis.

'I suppose not,' mused Dawlish, 'but they all react differently. What's that?' Dawlish peered into the trees.

It was nothing at all, but Dickerson did not know it; nor did he know that it was an invitation to him to try to escape. Hope deferred, in Dawlish's experience, was a very fine loosener of tongues. Dawlish and Felicity gazed in the opposite direction as Dickerson, glancing frantically about him, ran. The large man turned, almost lazily.

'He does all the obvious things, doesn't he?' He picked up a small, rotten branch of a tree, and tossed it in front of Dickerson, who went sprawling.

Dawlish sauntered towards him.

'All the obvious things,' he repeated, and then went on in a gentle but sincere enough voice: 'Dickerson, I don't want to hurt you, you know. In spite of what you have heard, I have my finer feelings. Where is my cousin?'

Sitting on the damp ground, Dickerson simply stared up at him.

'On the other hand,' said Dawlish in the same gentle voice, 'I'm quite prepared to do violence if you ask for it and I intend to learn where Sheila is, as well as one or two other things. So make up your mind. It can be the easy way or the hard one. It's up to you.'

'She—she won't be hurt,' muttered Dickerson, 'I assure you of that, Dawlish, you—you're making a fuss about nothing!'

'Oh, well,' said Dawlish. He bent down and yanked the man to his feet, and as he did so Felicity called to him in a quiet but compelling voice:

'Pat, someone's near by.'

Dawlish did not look round, but Dickerson sent a frightened glance about him and then emitted a single high-pitched screech.

'Help!' he cried, but a second call died in his throat as Dawlish moved his hand.

They waited in silence.

Presently Dawlish heard footsteps, or what he thought were

footsteps. Whoever was near had no intention of trying to hide his presence.

Dawlish said quietly:

'Don't call out again, Dickerson.'

The man did not, and the stranger continued to force a way through the undergrowth. Dawlish saw him, suddenly—and also saw the gun he was carrying; at a distance and through the trees it looked like a rifle. Dawlish put his left hand to his pocket, clasping the automatic which Dickerson had 'lost' the previous night.

Then the man reached the lane along which they had driven and, whistling as if unaware of anything unusual, stepped into the clearing. The 'rifle' was a shot-gun, which looked very old. The stranger was a youngish man, with curly hair falling over his forehead and a well-cut coat. He was wearing riding breeches and leather gaiters. The shot-gun was tucked beneath his arm; and over it dangled a brace of rabbits.

He stopped short at sight of the trio, but Dawlish, watching him closely, did not think that he looked surprised. It was Dawlish himself who was surprised when the man nodded to Dickerson.

It was none other than Sheila's young man with the milk. 'I thought I saw a car turn in here.' He bowed slightly towards Felicity but continued to eye Dickerson with obvious amusement, not untinged with malice.

Unless this was superb acting on the part of the stranger and Dickerson, these two men were bad friends and Dickerson could expect no sympathy, Dawlish decided.

'Can I help you at all?' the young man asked, politely. 'I mean, if you're lost—'

'The truth is,' said Dawlish, 'that we came here for a private talk with Dickerson—whom, I assume, you know?'

'You could say that,' said the young man with a smile, 'but

don't let me delay you, I'm sure that you are anxious to get on with the job.'

'Who told you about me?' asked Dawlish, slowly.

'Oh, a friend of a friend,' said the young man. 'I deliver the milk and so I know the baker, the butcher, and all the rest of them. It's surprising how things get around.' He eyed Dickerson curiously. 'I suppose,' he added tentatively, 'I can't offer to help?'

Dawlish said: 'You might, at that.' He took the automatic from his pocket and for the first time the young man looked startled; instinctively he moved the shot-gun, as if to protect himself. He did not move it far, for Dawlish handed the gun to Felicity.

'Keep him covered, in case he runs,' he said. 'I want a talk with the milkman.' He released Dickerson, who tottered to a fallen tree and sat down heavily.

Dawlish reached the milkman. 'I hope you don't mind me saying you rather puzzle me. I mean, if a law-abiding citizen saw another citizen being ill-treated or about to be ill-treated, I would have expected him to make some protest. Why don't you?'

'You've misjudged me,' said the milkman, mildly. 'If I thought you were going to hurt a hair of his head, I—' he smiled. 'I would hurry away so that I couldn't hear him squawk!'

'Ah,' said Dawlish. 'Not a friend of yours?'

'That puts it mildly.'

'Any particular reason?'

'Oh well, there's the way he dresses and the company he keeps—to say nothing of his reputation,' said the young man. 'I've known him for eighteen months and it's eighteen months too long. I knew that one day someone would tackle him. If I'd had half a chance I would have done it myself,' he added. 'By the way, my name's Corbett—Bruce Corbett, of Grange Farm.'

'Mine's Dawlish.'

'How d'you do?' said the other. 'I saw you coming here and caught a glimpse of Dickerson's face. After that I couldn't resist coming to see what was happening. I suppose I mustn't ask questions. I mean—you've some personal grudge against Dickerson, I take it?'

'Ye-es,' said Dawlish. 'Do you own Grange Farm?'

'I wish I did! No, I'm at a small cottage not far away from it—they call me the dairy manager, but that's simply because old Simpson is a kindly soul and likes me to think that I'm worth my salary!' Corbett's frankness was almost embarrassing and Dawlish thought that it was because he rarely met anyone of his own kind to whom he could talk. It was either that, or because he wanted to create an impression, and Dawlish preferred the first premise. 'Why, are you heading for the farm?'

Slowly, Dawlish shook his head.

'No. I'm looking for a secluded spot where Dickerson could have bed-and-breakfast for a night or two—longer if necessary.'

'Bed-and-breakfast!' gasped Corbett. 'But—'

'If you've been here for eighteen months you know the peculiarities of the Grange,' said Dawlish. 'People disappear. A cousin of mine has disappeared. After all, share and share alike, don't you think?'

Corbett stared at him, his expression blank at first, and then breaking into the beginning of a smile.

'Well, what about it?' Dawlish repeated.

'I don't know about the breakfast,' said Corbett, 'but I can find him a bed.'

'Counting all the risks?' asked Dawlish.

'What risks?'

'Don't tell me that you can't see any,' said Dawlish. 'Item one, if Dickerson is discovered at your place or gets away, he would be able to prefer a charge against us and get us both locked up. He's usually had his own way with the police so far, from what I've heard. Item two, he has friends. I don't know how many, but I can count up to two at least. They might investigate. I hope I'm making myself clear.'

'You're putting it very lucidly,' Corbett assured him. 'I'll take the risks, Dawlish—on one condition.'

'Ah, the snag,' said Dawlish.

'I hope you won't think so. For my help, your story.'

Dawlish's eyes creased at the corners.

'You'll do!' he said. 'All right, Corbett, but we'll have to think up ways and means of getting him to your cottage. Is it far? And can we get in without being seen?'

'It's about half-a-mile away and we can get there by car,' said Corbett. 'There's another copse like this immediately behind it and the nearest building is the farm. They're not working on any of the fields near the cottage today—it'll be sheer bad luck if anyone sees us. Unless'—he paused—'you seriously think that we might be watched.'

'We'd be foolish to overlook the possibility,' said Dawlish, 'but I think we might get away with it. We'd better let Dickerson know,' he added, 'he'll be in a panic by the time we get back. He might even be prepared to talk.'

Dickerson was made of sterner stuff than Dawlish had hoped; even further threats of violence would not make him disclose where Sheila had gone. However, they got him to Corbett's cottage without much difficulty. Between them, they carried him up the narrow stairs, Dawlish pushing a handkerchief into his mouth, when he attempted to shout.

At the head of the stairs, Corbett, who looked pale and appeared to have lost much of his tan, nearly dropped the man's legs. Dawlish eyed the other curiously.

'All right, I'll manage him,' he said.

Breathing hard, Corbett stood by the door of a small bedroom and watched Dawlish set to work, using a second handkerchief to tie round Dickerson's mouth. Next, Dawlish took a coil of cord from his hip pocket, cut a length off, and proceeded to bind Dickerson's wrists behind him. Then he lifted him bodily onto the bed, and made a neat job of tying his ankles. Dawlish tested the knots, stood back and surveyed his handiwork with detached interest, then took off Dickerson's shoes. He carried them with him downstairs, where Felicity was sitting in a rocking chair in a small, bright kitchen where brasses shone and the grate was polished like a mirror.

'Well, that's the first stage,' he said, 'the next is probably coming fairly soon, because they'll know that I took him away and they'll want to interview me. I wonder whether we'd better go to the *George*, Fel, or back to Wood Grange?'

'There's a little bargain, remember,' Corbett told him.

'I haven't forgotten. Can we decide on the course of action first?' asked Dawlish. When Corbett nodded he went on thoughtfully: 'If we have any luck, the house will be empty except for servants and we could have a look through it. I think that'll be worth trying,' he added, 'and afterwards—can you get to the *George* about two o'clock, Corbett? Or half past, if that would suit you better?'

Corbett shook his head regretfully.

'I can't get away until five, I'm afraid—I have a couple of hours off now, but that's all I can count on.' He explained that the dairy of Grange Farm was about a mile across country from the cottage, and added that he thought Dawlish could rely on help, within reason, from Farmer Simpson and his wife, who had no better opinion of Dickerson than Corbett himself.

'"Within reason" meaning—provided we don't involve them

in a police inquiry,' Dawlish hazarded. 'I think we'd better keep them out of it, unless we're in a corner.' He eyed Corbett thoughtfully. 'What kind of a place is the farm?'

'Oh, very good,' said Corbett. 'It's better than most and the Simpsons are really a decent couple. Why?'

'It might prove a better operational centre than the *George*,' said Dawlish. 'We'll think about it. But I don't like the idea of you waiting for the story until this evening, I'd better give you the general outline.' He did so, quickly and concisely—omitting only that he had first been introduced to the affair by Scotland Yard.

Corbett listened, his expression gradually changing. He was frowning when Dawlish finished. After a few moments silence he said quietly:

'So the girl I saw this morning is your cousin, and she's disappeared?' He looked evenly at Dawlish and went on: 'You shouldn't have let her take the risk, Dawlish, you should have known better.'

'I'm beginning to think so,' said Dawlish. 'Nevertheless, Sheila will be all right while we've got Dickerson, and because that will cause a minor crisis in the Dickerson camp, I think we can say that we're making progress.' He stood up. 'Before I go, just one question.'

Sharp on his words came the sound of a car engine. With one accord they all moved towards the window as a large black limousine pulled up. The car doors were flung open, revealing a chauffeur of somewhat forbidding aspect, and Dr. Brett.

CHAPTER TWELVE

DAWLISH LOOKS AROUND

In so great a hurry were Brett and his chauffeur that they did not notice the three people crowding in the window. Dawlish glanced at Corbett, who had gone pate—Dawlish frowned at that, his curiosity about the man growing apace. He did not allow it to influence his course of action however, and as the doctor banged on the front door, said quietly:

'Corbett, will you stay here with Felicity? Don't go out into the passage, let 'em break the door down or otherwise enter feloniously. It would be a good idea to have this door open and bang it to, as soon as they get into the passage.'

Corbett eyed him speculatively, but went up in the big man's estimation because he did not ask questions.

'All right,' he said.

'Don't hesitate to shoot to scare 'em,' Dawlish advised Felicity.

There was a loud banging on the front door as if the intention was to frighten the occupants by noise alone. Dawlish pushed the window wide open; what sound it made was drowned by the commotion from the front. The chauffeur, he saw, was putting his shoulder to the panels. Dawlish heard the agitated voice of Brett.

'Can't you get it open? Go round the back and try—'

The cottage door, not being made for such assaults, cracked with a noise like a pistol shot as it gave way; Dawlish thought that one or both of the men fell into the passage. He climbed through the window, and walked towards the front door.

The chauffeur was picking himself up and Brett was hammering with his clenched fist on the door of the room where Felicity and Corbett were waiting.

'There's someone here, I heard it bang,' he cried. 'I heard—'

'*Bang! Bang!*' cried Dawlish, in a loud voice.

Brett jumped violently and swung round. His fear was gone, probably lost in the white-hot rage possessing him—perhaps in a greater fear of someone other than Dawlish. The chauffeur swore, and strode towards Dawlish, in no way intimidated by the big man's stature.

'Dawlish!' cried Brett. 'Where is Dickerson? Where is—'

'The new housekeeper?' Dawlish finished for him, and had the satisfaction of making the man gulp. But the chauffeur still came forward threateningly. Probably he expected to intimidate the other by his manner alone, for he made no immediate attempt to strike Dawlish.

'Dawlish!' Brett's voice quivered. 'You took Dickerson away from his house, and you were seen. Unless you tell me where he is, I shall report immediately to the police!'

'Good idea,' Dawlish drawled. 'I'm sure they will be interested to meet you. You see, Mr. Corbett has a complaint to make, doctor. He dislikes people rushing at his front door and breaking it down. It comes under the legal phrase "felonious entry" and might even be construed into assault. Also, there is a question of damages. A police matter, undoubtedly,' he added, soberly. 'I'm surprised at you, you've always been so careful to avoid offending the police. Has something upset you?'

'See here—' began the chauffeur.

'Be quiet, Green!' Brett forced his way past the man.

'You cannot intimidate me!' he snapped. 'You kidnapped Dickerson and I am justified—'

'Oh, no,' said Dawlish, 'you're not justified in recoursing to violence, you should have asked the police to act. Don't make any mistake about it, Brett, you've broken the law and can be sent to jail for it.'

'You were seen—'

Dawlish shook his head reproachfully. 'I think you've gone to pieces, Brett, you shouldn't bring your gorillas about with you, you shouldn't break down the doors of other people's property.'

The chauffeur cleared his throat.

'Let me—' he began.

'Be quiet, Green!' Brett glanced up as the passage door opened, and Corbett and Felicity appeared. Corbett, receiving a nod from Dawlish, launched into a tirade against Brett and his chauffeur, making much of the damage and declaring that he would have immediate recourse to law. As he went on, waxing more and more indignant, Dawlish warmed towards him.

At last Corbett stopped.

'And so you see,' said Dawlish, shaking his head, 'you have been very foolish, Brett. Of course Corbett is angry—I wish there were a telephone here,' he added wistfully, 'we could have the police up in no time.' He smiled at Corbett. 'Don't worry,' he said reassuringly, 'they'll make good the damage.'

'*Where is Dickerson?*' shouted Brett.

'Where indeed?' said Dawlish, blandly. 'Of course he might be lost, but on the other hand he might have gone back to Wood Grange. Who knows? After all, Sheila Lynd went for a walk in the grounds, he told me, but she might find her way back, too. If one can, the other can, don't you think?'

'Oh,' said Brett, quietly, 'so *that's* it.'

'That's it,' said Dawlish, cheerfully. 'We may find that there's been a lot of fuss about nothing. I accused Dickerson of spiriting Sheila away and he denied it. If she came back Dickerson might reappear'—he beamed—'and we might even arrange to pacify Corbett by paying him for the damage, plus a little as earnest for future good behaviour. Say a hundred pounds.'

Brett brushed his hand across his forehead and said in a low-pitched voice.

'If Miss Lynd returns, can you guarantee that Dickerson will?'

'Now, come,' protested Dawlish, 'how can I guarantee it when I don't know where Dickerson is? I'll agree to this though; if you send out search parties to look for Sheila, I'll send others out to look for Dickerson, and who knows, we might both be successful.'

'If you ask me,' said the chauffeur drily, 'Mr. Dickerson isn't far from *here*.'

Dawlish beamed. 'Well, that's reasonable enough—he can't have gone far, unless he got a lift in a milk lorry.'

Brett started; Corbett drew a deep breath, and Felicity looked at him quickly. Brett drew his hand across his forehead, then turned his head and said to Green:

'Come along, Green.'

'But—' began the chauffeur.

'Do as you're told!' snapped Brett. Reluctantly, Green followed him, glaring at Dawlish as he passed.

After the storm of their arrival, their departure was an anticlimax. Soberly they took their seats and the big car disappeared in the direction of Terne.

'Dawlish,' said Corbett, 'I hand it to you—that was the slickest piece of work I've seen in my life!'

Dawlish smiled. 'You're a bit extravagant, aren't you?' he

asked. 'A simple problem, after all—I just stated terms. Brett assumed that I would have been much more alarmed had Dickerson been at the cottage, so he hurried off to tell his master that (a) he has been fool enough to give the police a chance to convict him (b) that I've offered Dickerson in return for Sheila.'

'His master?' Corbett queried.

'Well, obviously.'

'I hadn't thought that there was anyone else,' said Corbett, 'but you may be right. Do you always work at speed like this?'

'It depends how fast the horse will go!' said Dawlish.

'I suppose so,' said Corbett, frowning a little. 'I say, Dawlish—what was that crack of yours about a milk lorry?'

Dawlish told Corbett exactly what had happened on the drive of Wood Grange and of his suspicion that the milk lorry driver had not been wholly unaware of the plan. Corbett looked sceptical.

'I don't think you're right there, Dawlish. It would be the morning lorry, collecting from the various farms—it was up at Grange Farm as usual. It's one of a fleet of transport vehicles used by the West Country Milk Supply Company. No one in a job like that would have anything to do with a racket.'

Dawlish shrugged. 'Perhaps not, he might just have heard the M.G. and been curious. On the other hand, Brett didn't like the reference, did he?'

'He was scared all right,' said Corbett.

'So you saw that, too,' mused Dawlish. 'Oh, well, we're making progress of a kind. You're sure that you're not free for the afternoon? You might be a help.'

'I might be able to get Simpson to spare me for the rest of the day,' Corbett said, reflectively. 'He dislikes everything belonging to Dickerson and would gladly see him in jail!'

'No brotherly spirit?' murmured Dawlish.

Corbett laughed, a little bitterly.

'None! People on this side of Terne haven't any love for Dickerson and his friends.'

'Which is the question I was going to ask you a long time ago,' said Dawlish. 'Why do the villagers dislike Dickerson?'

Corbett did not immediately reply, and when he did, the reasons seemed fairly trivial.

Dickerson, he said, was suspected of dodging war work or one of the Services; he also lived the life of a country gentleman without being one. There was, too, his attitude towards the local girls. There was nothing definite, nothing to take hold of, only this instinctive dislike and distrust.

'He's just built himself a reputation,' murmured Dawlish.

'Ye-es. Do you think he's intended to?' asked Corbett.

'It could be, but I don't yet see the reason for it,' said Dawlish. 'Is that all?'

'Until this housekeeper business,' said Corbett. 'When the woman's body was found in the river, wearing the clothes of one of the housekeepers, there was an indignation meeting in the Square at Terne! Some of the brighter sparks seemed to think that the police were deliberately evading the issue, but the local newspapermen saw the body—it certainly wasn't one of Dickerson's women.'

'And that satisfied the angry populace?' mused Dawlish.

'Up to a point, but don't misunderstand me, Dawlish. There's always an energetic minority in a scandal like this. There's no doubt that a great deal of feeling against him has been worked up by agitation. It's made worse because he doesn't seem to care and flaunts himself, his staff, his life of ease, whenever he gets the chance.'

'Remarkable!' said Dawlish. 'Oh, well, it won't do him any

harm to stay upstairs a bit.' He frowned. 'Unless there's some-where else we could put him? We can hardly keep the cottage guarded all day, and Brett might have a look through and find him. It would be just as well to avoid any confrontation at this stage, and there is your reputation to consider.'

'I'm not worried about my reputation,' said Corbett, stoutly, 'but it would be a pity to lose him now. There's nowhere but the copse, I'm afraid—well, there *is* a ditch running through it just behind the house, an anti-tank trap that they dug in 1940. It would be mere chance if anyone happened to come across him there.'

'Good!' Dawlish moved towards the stairs again, 'an excellent idea.'

The transfer of the prisoner from the cottage to the tank trap took little more than ten minutes and then the trio went back to the M.G. As they reached it, Corbett laughed, for no apparent reason.

'Now what's the matter?' asked Dawlish.

'I'm just beginning to realise how completely detached you are!' exclaimed Corbett. 'Most men would have made an enor-mous fuss and bother and be scared stiff in case the police discovered him.'

Dawlish shrugged. 'Blame my black past,' he said. 'Will you try to get the afternoon off?'

'Yes.'

'Good! I'll look in at Wood Grange and then come along to the farm,' said Dawlish. 'If you've managed it, we can go to Terne together. I'd like you to join in,' he added, quietly, 'because I'm going to need someone who knows the district well and has the proper outlook.'

Corbett chuckled. 'I've the proper outlook all right!'

He gave them directions to the farm for their return journey, and then Dawlish drove slowly back to Wood Grange. Felicity, who had shown a remarkable restraint throughout the morning's incidents, looked ahead of her, silent and undemanding. When they reached the main road and began to coast downhill, Dawlish looked at her appreciatively.

'Fel, there's no one quite like you!'

'I rather thought that myself.'

Dawlish laughed. 'If I don't manage to get this over so that we have a couple of days on our own, I'll give up!' They exchanged glances; for perhaps thirty seconds Dickerson, Sheila, Corbett, and all the rest were forgotten. Then a motor-cyclist roared past them and a small convoy of tanks and armoured cars followed. Dawlish straightened up, paid more attention to his driving and asked in a non-committal voice:

'What do you make of Corbett, Fel?'

'I don't quite know,' admitted Felicity.

'Meaning?'

'Well, he tried to hedge you off the milk lorry business,' Felicity said, thoughtfully, 'and I can't understand why he was quite so helpful. He *seems* all right—but he looked frightened once or twice—even to the point of losing colour.'

'Ye-es,' said Dawlish. 'I don't think the lost colour was fright, but simply strain. He puffed like a steam engine when we carried Dickerson up the stairs, although I took most of the weight. No, he's not fit, that's probably why he's working on the farm,' Dawlish went on. 'All the same, his behaviour *is* curious. He says he warned Sheila to get away. Could it be just because of the general feeling against Dickerson, I wonder, or is there something else?'

'I don't know,' said Felicity, looking a little sheepish. 'I feel rather mean about suspecting him!'

'So do I,' admitted Dawlish, 'but we mustn't take anyone on his face value. The milk lorry angle might be worth following up,' he added, 'and I'd better see the police for an analysis of that stuff they were going to pump into you. One thing we can claim,' he added, with satisfaction, 'is that we've forced things to move a bit, and now we'll see what kind of reception we get at the Grange. If Brett's there we won't stay long, but if there's only the staff, we'll have a look round.'

The front door of the Grange was open.

That was not particularly surprising, since the day was warm, but the sight of Maude standing on the porch, wringing her hands and then raising them towards the heavens as if in supplication was certainly unusual.

Dawlish pulled up and jumped out of the car. Maude's face was haggard, her hair was dishevelled, and it was obvious she had been crying. She must have seen Dawlish but she took no notice of him at all.

'I told her,' she moaned, 'I told her, I told her!'

Dawlish said, gently: 'What is it, Maude?'

'I told her, I told her!' moaned Maude, and at last looked at him with tragic eyes. 'I'm not staying here another minute, not another minute!'

Dawlish forced himself to control a rising anxiety.

'Who did you tell? Who are you talking about?'

'Miss Lynd!' cried Maude, 'she's gone! She was running away, and she fell over the hill to her death. And I told her to go away, I told her!'

Dawlish said sternly: 'Stop that moaning! Tell me quietly what happened.'

'She ran out of the trees and then she fell!' cried Maude. 'Over there—the others are looking for her.'

Dawlish turned and stared towards the wall which surrounded Wood Grange. Beyond it was a grassy slope and a group of trees. Near them two maids were standing and gesticulating. Except for Maude's sniffing there was a strange silence everywhere, an emptiness which affected Dawlish so that he, too, stood silent for an appreciable moment.

Then he spoke harshly.

'Fel, make Maude get you some ropes. Maude—have the police been told?'

'The gardener's gone to tell them, the 'phone won't work,' muttered Maude, her sniffs diminishing at the prospect of action. 'The rope's in the shed, m'm, I'll show you—'

Felicity followed Maude, while Dawlish hurried towards the wall, leapt over its five feet, then sprinted across the meadow towards the two maids still staring into the distance and waving their arms. Here the ground dropped sharply away. Rugged boulders of rock were strewn about the upper slopes. From the edge of these, the land fell steeply and immediately below them was the river.

CHAPTER THIRTEEN

THE LONG DESCENT

Moving cautiously, Dawlish went down the upper slopes, catching at boulders and stunted trees. Twenty yards or so below him he could see what looked like a leather handbag. When he was a little nearer, he saw that it was just that. Each time he stepped downward his heels slipped, for the grass, growing thinly over rock, gave little support. He pictured Sheila running headlong from her pursuers, reaching the top and then slipping.

He could imagine her falling.

He reached the handbag but did not pick it up. The going grew more difficult, but there were enough boulders to give him purchase and, a little lower, there was a ledge on which he would be able to stand. He reached it and stood swaying there when Felicity's voice, carried high in the wind, reached him.

'Pat! *Pat!*'

Cautiously he looked up. The ledge, as slippery as the rest of the grass-covered patches, was no more than a foot wide. Even from where he was standing he could not see more than half-a-dozen feet down the side of the hill.

Felicity was coiling a rope above her head.

'All right!' called Dawlish.

She flung the rope, which uncoiled itself and came towards him, falling about ten feet to his right. Carefully he made his way towards it; when he had it in his hand, he saw that Felicity had tied one end to a tree at the top; she was pointing to it, to make sure that he realised what she had done.

'That's fine!' he called. 'Any more rope?'

'Some coming!'

Perhaps because of the height and the panorama Dawlish was not aware of any sense of depression. Nor could he bring himself to believe that Sheila had fallen to her death. A strange exhilaration possessed him, but that went as he faced the practical difficulties. Turning his back on the sheer drop, he began to lower himself.

There was no sign of Sheila.

Tight-lipped, because he knew that if she had fallen farther than he could see there was little hope for her, he went down another twenty feet, until he reached the second of the rocky ledges. It was a relief to feel the solid rock beneath him and to be able to stand upright. He had little slack left in the rope, if he had to venture farther he would have to do it on his own.

Then he saw Sheila!

She was pressed against a wall of cliff not very far below him. She waved tremulously.

'Pat!' she cried. 'Pat!'

'Hallo, hallo!' boomed Dawlish, 'what kind of a trick do you call this?'

'I'm all right!'

'So I should think!' He surveyed her position, marvelling at the fact that she had fallen to a jutting, shrub covered piece of rock. The undergrowth had obviously broken her fall. Nor was there any immediate danger. He was so delighted that at first he considered waiting until more help arrived. He was about to call down and tell her that the police were coming when he saw a little cloud of dust rise from the side of the rock where she was standing. She appeared to notice nothing, but looked startled at Dawlish's change of expression.

'What is it, Pat?'

He called: 'Stay there, I'm coming down!' He put his hands to his lips, and roared to Felicity. 'Throw the other rope!' he cried. 'Throw the rope!' He felt a desperate sense of urgency but did not want to alarm Sheila, although he knew that someone was firing at her, probably from the side of the hill not very far away. 'Throw the rope!' he repeated and his voice echoed about the hill.

He could see Felicity's head above the cliff edge. As the second rope slithered down he was able to catch it.

'Pat!'

Sheila's voice, a mingled cry of alarm and surprise, drifted up to him. He turned and saw her staring towards the opposite hill—and immediately afterwards another little chipping fell away from the rock. She turned her head and he saw that all the colour had fled from her cheeks.

'Pat, someone's shooting.' He just heard the words.

'They won't for long,' he encouraged her, looping the rope before tossing it down to her. 'Put it round your waist, and—'

He thought he heard the crack of a shot, but there was no mistaking the way Sheila stumbled towards the edge of the rock. She looked as if she would fall, and he saw that there was a red mark on the shoulder of her blouse.

She said nothing, but crouched low.

'Good sense,' thought Dawlish, approvingly, but he was filled with an increasing tension as he watched her slip the rope about her waist.

94

At last, she called:

'I'm ready, Pat.'

With great courage she stood upright, bracing her body as she waited for Dawlish to haul her upwards.

With no room in which to manoeuvre, and conscious of the possibility that the snipers would change their target, Dawlish began to pull. Inch by inch Sheila moved up. The weight was considerable, even for him, and he knew that one serious slip would be enough to send them both downwards.

It seemed an age, but was actually only five minutes before he was able to drag her on to his ledge.

Breathing heavily, Sheila dead white and Dawlish red with exertion, they stood together, unable to move more than a few inches on either side, the steep slope behind them, the sheer drop in front.

'Well, we're half-way home at all events,' said Dawlish with an unexpected grin. 'How's that shoulder?' It was a superfluous question, for the blouse had been torn away in the climb, and he could see that although the wound had bled freely it was not serious. 'They can't shoot for nuts, can they?' he said.

'Don't!' exclaimed Sheila.

He gripped her hand. 'It's grim, of course, but you've done marvels, you know. I don't believe that the luck will turn against us now that it's gone our way for so long. I wish the police would hurry, all the same!'

Both of them realised that their immunity from shooting might be short-lived, as they stood exposed on that bleak hillside.

Beyond him, towards the right in the direction of Terne, Dawlish saw two cars moving along the road and he liked to imagine that the police were in them. Then he heard a slight sound, and a few seconds later a tell-tale chipping flew from a piece of rock not a yard away from him. Sheila noticed it, but said nothing. Simultaneously they bent down, but there was hardly room and they would not be able to stay like that for long. Dawlish, so impotent now, felt less afraid than bitterly angry.

'What led up to this?' he asked, in an endeavour to take Sheila's mind off the immediate danger.

'I—I went for a walk in the grounds and fell into a hole.' Sheila looked over her shoulder nervously, but went on talking. 'It wasn't a big one, but obviously it's a hiding-place for something. There were one or two bags there. It was all covered over—the surface, I mean—with bracken and shrubs. Then I tried to get out, but there wasn't much chance and I stayed there until—'

A bullet passed between their faces. They felt the wind and stared at each other, startled; it was as if an angry wasp had flicked the ends of their noses.

Then they heard the sound of an engine.

Dawlish looked upwards—and he heard shouting. It was impossible to distinguish between one voice and another but obviously there was a great alarm up above. The note of the engine grew deeper; it was a powerful one and it's throb was heavy. It seemed to beat through the very cliff. He straightened up and Sheila did the same, while the ledge on which they stood began to tremble.

The shouting was now lost in the roar and clatter which came from above their heads. Dawlish, craning his neck painfully, saw pieces of rock and dirt begin to fall—but they were all fifty feet or more away. He knew that if others came from immediately above the ledge they would have no chance of surviving at all.

The noise itself was frightening, but the gradually increasing avalanche of dirt and trees, shrubs and rock, falling down the side of the hill, was ten times more so. Then something else appeared, feeling its way with grotesque timidity about the top of the hill—but there was nothing timid about it's appearance; dark and menacing it rose against the skyline.

It was a tank; nothing more nor less than an army tank. It's great tractors loomed over the precipice as it began to feel its way forward, but nothing on wheels could come down such a slope without toppling. Yet for what seemed an endless time it nosed about, spewing dirt and rock from beneath its tractors, sometimes threatening to come immediately towards them, at others pointing in the opposite direction. With nerve-racking slowness more of it came into sight; half of it, thought Dawlish, with a cold weight in the pit of his stomach.

Then the tank began to fall.

CHAPTER FOURTEEN

THE TANK THAT RAN AMOK

It did not fall immediately towards them, but it was no more than thirty feet to the left, lurching from side to side, its tractors still making a pretence of clinging to the earth. Then, as they watched, it seemed to turn a lazy but monstrous somersault in slow-motion. Dawlish, his stomach ice-cold, was not aware of Sheila's hands gripping his arm as both of them stared upward. The din was deafening, for the engine was still roaring.

A large boulder broke away and went hurtling down the hillside. Small pieces of rubble fell about them, one smacking sharply against the side of Dawlish's face. Then the tank drew level with them, gathering sickening speed. A moment later it had disappeared, but the avalanche of dirt and rock and scrub which followed increased, while a cloud of dust rose up and made a pall about them.

The hideous noise faded gradually.

The dust remained, floating thickly about their heads. Now that the worst had passed Dawlish grew aware of the painful pressure of Sheila's fingers. She said nothing, but gulped down a lump in her throat.

'The dust is a help, because no one can see us and they won't waste their bullets,' said Dawlish comfortingly. 'In fact they'll take it for granted that the tank has done their job for them, so there'll be no more trouble.' He remembered the little convoy which had been on the road, yet it seemed incredible that Dickerson or his friends had contrived to send a tank over the brow of the hill; it was equally incredible that they had a tank to send.

'All we need do,' he added, 'is to wait.' When Sheila did not answer, he went on: 'We shall probably spend all the afternoon drinking! Beer for me, tea for you!'

The tremor in Sheila's hands steadied, and she even contrived to smile a little, although with an obvious effort.

'Weren't you saying that you were in a hole and there was no way out?' Dawlish went on.

'Er—yes, I was,' said Sheila. 'It was just past the wall of the grounds—not very far from a gate. I thought I'd better not stay too near you, because Dickerson might think that we were too friendly.'

'He does!' smiled Dawlish, 'but that doesn't matter and it will keep. What about this hidey-hole of yours?'

'Well, I began to shout for help,' said Sheila. 'It was very quiet and I don't think my voice travelled very far, although it sounded loud enough in the pit! Then I heard footsteps. Someone dropped a cloth over my head. It fell over my shoulders and I couldn't get it off. I—I was frightened out of my wits!'

'That's not surprising,' said Dawlish stoutly.

'Don't you ever feel scared?' asked Sheila.

'Nearly every day of my life,' Dawlish assured her extravagantly.

'You weren't scared just now.'

'But I wouldn't like to think I was going to experience the

same five minutes again—not for a fortune!' He grinned. 'Let's get on with the story. Someone dropped a cloth over your head and so you were blindfolded. Then—'

'A man jumped into the pit,' said Sheila. 'I know it was a man, although I didn't see him. He gripped my ankles and raised me upwards. He didn't say a word. Someone on the edge of the pit gripped my wrists and hauled me up. Then someone came running up to say that you were coming—he seemed alarmed!'

'That's a help,' said Dawlish, 'because we may be able to worry 'em again. And then?'

'They forgot about me for a moment,' said Sheila, 'and I managed to get the cloth off and run. The men started to follow me, but I had a few yards start and they were still thinking about you—but for that I don't think I would have been able to get away. Then I heard one of them say: "*Let her go*".' She paused, and Dawlish nodded, gently.

'The next thing I knew was that I was falling over the cliff.'

She shrugged. 'That's all—I landed on the ledge.'

She looked down on the dark slope of earth and rock, knowing the luck that had been hers. One inch to the right— One inch to the left—.

She shuddered.

'Just a little matter of coincidence,' Dawlish said hastily. 'They're taking long enough to get here, aren't they?'

'It doesn't matter now,' said Sheila.

They waited for perhaps another quarter of an hour before ropes were lowered from the top of the precipice. Dawlish fastened one around Sheila's waist and watched as she was pulled up. It was not long before he followed.

Aware only of Felicity at first, Dawlish soon grew conscious of the fact that a crowd of thirty or forty people had gathered there, including a reporter and a cameraman. A plain-clothes man came forward and introduced himself, with a tentative smile, as Inspector Bligh.

'I'm glad you people didn't lose much time,' Dawlish said. 'Smart work.'

'It's not the first time we've had trouble over this hill,' Bligh said soberly. To Dawlish, there seemed to be something behind the man's words. 'I'm very glad it was no worse, Mr. Dawlish.'

'Mutual congratulations,' murmured Dawlish. 'Shall we—'

He stopped, abruptly.

Sheila was standing a few yards away, assuring Bruce Corbett—who had just arrived on foot—that she was all right, while a tall woman in a Red Cross uniform attended to her shoulder.

Suddenly, terrifyingly, there was the crack of a shot. The nurse uttered a gasp, staggered and began to fall. Corbett jumped to her side while Dawlish began to run, with Bligh and other policemen, towards a patch of trees no more than fifty feet away.

As he ran, his knees felt weak and he knew that the episode on the cliff had taken a lot out of him. He had to let the others go ahead, and for fear of hampering them, turned back. Felicity and Sheila were on their knees beside the nurse.

As Dawlish drew up he saw that nothing could be done. He approached, sombre-faced, knowing that had Sheila not moved to speak to Bruce Corbett the bullet would have entered the back of her head. Instead it was the Red Cross nurse who had been killed.

The police failed to find the murderer, who, presumably taking advantage of a better knowledge of the countryside, had escaped through the trees and reached one of the many narrow lanes which meandered about the hills over-looking Terne. When

Bligh and his men came back, Dawlish led them to the hidden pit in which Sheila had fallen. But it was empty, although there were traces of a white powder and a slightly acrid smell.

'Did you see his face?' asked Bligh.

'Not clearly,' Dawlish told him. 'The sun was shining on him, but I got the impression of a little fellow with a pointed nose. A good marksman, too—better than the others.'

Bligh looked startled.

'Oh, there were others,' said Dawlish, grimly, 'but before we go into that I want to get the girls into Terne under a close guard. They might not be in any immediate danger, since her would-be murderer would assume that Sheila would have told her story by now. Still, I don't altogether like the way things are going.'

'What was her story?' asked Bligh.

'You know nearly as much as I do,' said Dawlish. 'Shall we get back to Terne first? I need a bath and a change. Afterwards, if I may, I'll come along and see you.'

'Delighted,' Bligh said. 'I knew that you were coming, of course.'

Dawlish raised an eyebrow.

'So Bill Trivett's been confidential, has he? Dare I ask what arrangements you're going to make up here?'

Bligh told him that, where possible, Special Constables and Army and Home Guard units would be used to comb the countryside for the murderer; there would be a widespread search for other small pits. The powder would be analysed, everyone living within a reasonable radius would be questioned—particularly Dickerson and his servants and Dr. Brett.

'So Bligh doesn't know that Dickerson's vanished into thin air,' thought Dawlish. 'Brett hasn't reported it yet.' He was glad, preferring to deal with Brett himself, preferring also to have Dickerson where he could interrogate him personally. Once the police knew that Dickerson had been man-handled, there would be a rumpus; the niceties of the English law would make that unavoidable. On the available evidence the police could be no more than suspicious and they were not likely to force the issue too far even if Brett made a complaint. If they proved their case, however, Dawlish would have some difficult explaining to do.

He decided that it would be wiser to say nothing of Brett's intrusion at Corbett's cottage.

An ambulance took the body of the nurse away, Sheila went ahead in a police car, with Felicity, and Dawlish drove Bligh to the *George*. He had had an opportunity for a word with Corbett, who had succeeded in getting the afternoon off, and who was to see him at the *George* at half past four. It was then a little before two o'clock.

As Dawlish followed in the wake of the police car, he shot a sideways glance at the Terne policeman, who remained somewhat solid of aspect if shrewd of eye. Bligh caught the glance and allowed himself a slow smile.

'Deep thoughts?' asked Dawlish.

'I was thinking what a clever devil he is,' said Bligh, without much show of feeling.

'Ah. Dickerson?'

'Of course. Now that they have been forced to come into the open, it's all happened *outside* his grounds. Until we find a direct connection between the pit, for instance, and Wood Grange, we can do nothing about Dickerson.'

Dawlish shrugged. 'Oh, he's clever.' He reflected that even Sheila's story told the same tale—her misadventures had taken place outside the walls. The trivial charge Corbett would be able to bring against Brett might, eventually, be useful, but it would be a waste of time to bring it up now. 'Why isn't the house watched, Bligh?'

'It was,' said Bligh, slowly, 'but Superintendent Trivett advised me to remove my men as soon as you arrived.'

'Oh,' said Dawlish, and smiled to himself; Trivett had known that he would probably take liberties with the law and considered it wiser not to allow him to become involved with the local police, who would be less likely to turn a blind eye towards his unorthodox activities. 'Not a bad idea,' went on Dawlish. 'Thoughtful of him!'

'I didn't ask why,' said Bligh, drily.

'Perhaps it's as well,' said Dawlish. 'So all you have of Dickerson are suspicions?'

'We've never been able to catch him out on even a trivial point of law yet,' said Bligh. 'If we had done so, we'd be able to get a search-warrant and go through the house, but I doubt whether he keeps anything incriminating there. I don't mind admitting that Dickerson is a nightmare to me—*and* to all of us in Terne. We know the fellow is a rogue, but—' he broke off, helplessly. 'Well, what can we do?'

'Since when have you really been worried about him?' asked Dawlish.

'We've had our eye on him for some time, but the disappearing housekeepers gave us the first thing to bite on,' said Bligh. 'I almost danced a jig when I heard about the body in the river, I thought that would give us a reason for searching the house and perhaps forcing Dickerson into a corner, but now— *we* can't blame Dickerson because another woman wore the clothes of someone who once worked for him.'

'Have you identified the body?'

'Yes,' said Bligh, grimacing. 'We've had to come to the conclusion that it was suicide, too. Nothing pointed to foul play. She was in the Accounts Department of the local whole-sale dairy company, and it's been known for some time that there has been some pilfering. She was accused of it—there was no prosecution, but she was dismissed in the middle of the week. She was heard to threaten suicide.' Bligh shrugged. 'What can I do about that? I've seen Dickerson, but he just grinned at me. *Damn* the fellow!' added Bligh with feeling.

Dawlish said, as if casually:

'The local milk people, you say?'

'Yes—the South West Wholesale Dairy Company,' said Bligh. 'They treat their staff very decently—nine firms out of ten would have prosecuted her. The management is badly upset about what happened—they think that had they prosecuted they might have saved the girl's life. Still, that's a side-issue. What we want is the connection between Dickerson and the girl—and I just don't see any way of getting it.'

Dawlish wondered what Bligh would say if he knew that he, Dawlish, already suspected that a lorry driver of the same company was implicated. Deciding that it was even more necessary for him to keep his own counsel, he changed the subject. 'By the way—that tank?'

They were approaching the *George* and Bligh did not answer until Dawlish had pulled up in the courtyard.

'The tank was one of half-a-dozen which had been on manoeuvres,' Bligh said at last. 'It had broken down and was left near the top of the hill—'

Dawlish asked, sharply: 'Without a guard?'

'No, there was a guard,' said Bligh. 'He says that he heard a call for help and went to try to find out where it was coming from. Someone got into the tank and started it. He was seen jumping clear, just before it fell over the top, but he wasn't caught.'

'There couldn't have been much wrong with the tank,' Dawlish growled. 'Why did the ass leave it?'

Bligh shrugged as he said:

'There wasn't much the matter, but the tractor was loose on one side and they needed a spare pin. It was never so bad that it wouldn't start off. We've a thin clue, anyhow—whoever started it must know how to handle the controls.'

'Ye-es,' said Dawlish, 'but I doubt if that will help a great deal. Will you look after things here while I see how the girls are and have some lunch?'

Bligh agreed to this, while Dawlish went up to his room, finding Sheila, with her shoulder neatly bandaged, and Felicity sitting on the edge of the bed. They were in a quandary, because they had forgotten to get Sheila's clothes from Wood Grange.

'I'll see that they're brought here,' Dawlish assured them. 'In the meanwhile I'll have lunch sent up—take it easy and don't be surprised if you find flat-footed gentlemen following you about if you leave the place.'

Before awkward questions could be asked, Dawlish retired to the bathroom. Dressed and refreshed he appeared again as lunch was brought up and a table laid in the bedroom. Conversation could hardly be said to sparkle. Felicity spoke little, while Sheila admitted that she had slept so badly the night before that she felt tired out.

'Of course, the fall over the cliff had nothing to do with it,' said Dawlish. 'An invigorating experience, in fact!'

Sheila grimaced at him.

'Pat,' said Felicity, 'do the police know about Dickerson's disappearance?'

'Not yet, I hope they won't for a while; that is, until I have bargained with Dr. Brett! How I wish Ted and Tim were here,' he added, regretfully.

'Who are they?' inquired Sheila.

'Friends who have lent a hand from time to time,' said Dawlish, 'and have as little respect for authorised methods as I have! Yes, we could use 'em, but—your milkman seems a useful customer, Sheila. By the way, did he warn you not to stay at Wood Grange?'

'Yes. I wanted to tell you—' Sheila made good her omission of the morning. Dawlish was puzzled by the confirmation of Corbett's warning to Sheila; it appeared to prove the man's good will, but was it likely that, on such a chance encounter, a man would utter such a warning?

He wondered how best he could learn more about Corbett and decided that Bligh was his most likely informant.

He left the hotel soon after three o'clock, and found his way without any trouble to the police headquarters. He was not recognised until he gave his name, when a sergeant took him to a room on the first floor.

Bligh was sitting at his desk, but at sight of Dawlish he pulled up a comfortable armchair and pointed to a box of cigarettes at Dawlish's side.

'I'll have a pipe, thanks,' said Dawlish, looking about him.

On a corner of the desk there were two or three pieces of metal. He eyed them curiously, and Bligh looked at him and smiled.

'Souvenirs from a Nazi 'plane,' he said, 'we found a few bits and pieces in the district last week, but not the 'plane itself.'

'Blew up and scattered, I suppose,' said Dawlish.

'Probably. It was a big one, if the experts are any judge—a transport.' Bligh dismissed the subject with a wave of the hand, yet something in his manner made Dawlish very curious. He pondered for a few moments, but Bligh gave him no lead.

'Well, what do we know?' asked Dawlish.

'There isn't a great deal more I can tell you,' said Bligh. 'I only wish there were!'

'What mendacity,' murmured Dawlish.

'In fact, I was hoping,' continued Bligh, only to stop and frown as if he suddenly realised what Dawlish had said. 'What did you say?'

'I said "what mendacity",' Dawlish told him gently. 'I have met many policemen and learned something of their wiles.' He waved his pipe. 'Trivett tried to convince me that the police were completely flummoxed, but he should have known better. I hoped for a more generous attitude from you.'

Bligh sat rather more stiffly in his chair.

'I don't quite understand you, Major Dawlish.'

'Oh, no need for formality,' protested Dawlish. 'After all, I'm the Aunt Sally and I should know what's going to be shied at me!' He smiled gently. 'I suppose I can't expect you to tell me the whole truth, but at least you might admit that you're keeping something back.'

Bligh, very uncomfortable indeed, flushed a brick red.

'Oh, well,' said Dawlish, carelessly. 'There is something, of course. I suppose you suspect something very nasty, but you aren't sure and you don't want to commit yourself. Is that it?' He sighed when Bligh continued to keep silent. 'I should have known better than to expect you to answer,' he admitted, 'my childish faith in policemen remains firm in spite of many rebuffs. What do you know about Dr. Brett?'

Bligh gave a sigh of relief.

'Oh, the doctor! Not a great deal. He is a qualified practitioner—he used to have a practice in Terne and then he took up a commercial appointment out in the rural district. He didn't stay there long, but retired and bought the house next door to Dickerson. I think they were acquainted before Dickerson came here, three years before the war. If not, they're very good friends now.'

'Ye-es,' murmured Dawlish, who had given up all immediate

hope of persuading Bligh to talk frankly, 'friends or partners. So Brett is fairly well-known about here—and, presumably, respected?'

'Well, he *was*,' said Bligh slowly. 'But there is a lot of work for the five doctors left in Terne, three of them older men than Brett. He was asked to help them out, but refused. It didn't go down well with the locals.'

'So that disposes of Dr. Brett,' murmured Dawlish, 'except to ask whether you ever suspected that he worked with Dickerson?'

'We knew there was an association,' said Bligh, guardedly.

'H'm, yes. Well, what about a Mr. Bruce Corbett, who works at Grange Farm for a farmer and his wife—Simpson by name, I think. Yes, Simpson.'

Bligh looked puzzled. 'Why, what has Corbett done?'

'He's been very helpful and he dislikes Dickerson—I wondered if you had any idea of the reason.'

'I don't think you need look further than you've seen already for anyone's dislike of Dickerson,' Bligh said. 'As for Corbett—he's a very likeable young fellow and I feel sorry for him, for he's taken a lot of hard knocks well. He's the nephew of Sir Mortimer Calshott, who lives across the Somerset border. Naturally, he was expected to go into the family business, but apparently he fell out with his uncle and he went to London. He joined the R.A.F., was brought down over Germany in one of the leaflet raids and faced the prospect of being in a prisoner-of-war camp for the duration. He managed to escape after about eighteen months and got to England—but he was barely alive,' added Bligh, abruptly. 'He had spent six months getting across Europe under cover, and I doubt if he had had a square meal in all that time. He came down here to a nursing home—I think Sir Mortimer arranged it, although they're not on speaking terms—and of course the best thing for him is open air. He has to take things very quietly for a while. He knew the Simpsons and took the job they offered him—technically the dairy manager, actually a roundsman. He knows it, of course, but—well, if you've met him you know that there's no side tohim at all.'

'Certainly no side,' said Dawlish, thoughtfully.

'What makes you think he might be more than he appears to be?' asked Bligh, a little sharply.

'Oh, I don't! I wish he weren't quite so ready to dislike Dickerson, that's all. He's not the type to base his dislikes on hearsay, and I rather expected to hear that there was an old-standing quarrel.'

Bligh smiled. 'There is! Dickerson started to run a pony and trap when petrol rationing got really bad, but he made the mistake of trying to whip the pony when it wouldn't take a big load uphill. Dickerson was in a pretty fury when Corbett appeared. I think they came to blows. The pony now belongs to Corbett,' added Bligh, with a gesture which seemed to say: 'So you can see who won *that* round!' 'Dickerson hires a taxi—he has one of the Terne taxi-drivers in his pocket. He pays well, of course.'

'Have you a *Who's Who* on the station, Bligh?'

'A *Who's Who*? Yes, there's one in the library.'

Bligh telephoned for the book and Dawlish flipped the pages over to 'C'. He was not at all surprised to find that Sir Mortimer Calshott was the Managing Director of the South West Wholesale Dairy Company Limited, but Bligh appeared very puzzled indeed when Dawlish closed the book and stood up slowly, whistling to himself.

CHAPTER FIFTEEN

TASKS FOR TWO LADIES

'The police won't go all the way with us,' said Dawlish to Felicity, 'and so we do a little journeying by ourselves. That's if Sheila's fit enough?'

'I'm all right,' said Sheila, hastily.

Dawlish regarded her thoughtfully.

Something had happened to Sheila. It might be no more than the effect of wholesome fear and confession of it. It might be that the adventure at Wood Grange had lifted her out of herself, and pushed her unlucky love affair into a secondary place. Whatever it was, it had a most beneficial effect on her appearance, for in spite of her wounded shoulder, she looked fresh, eager, and very beautiful.

'That's fine,' said Dawlish. 'Corbett's coming here in half an hour or so and I'll probably go up to the farm with him and perhaps have a word with Dickerson, who should be in a more communicative frame of mind by then. Meanwhile, I've a burning desire to know more about the local office of the South West Wholesale Dairy Company Limited, its managing director, Sir Mortimer Calshott, its reputation, and the reputation and life of a girl who worked in the Accounts Office here—a Mildred Gay. An unlikely name,' he added gently, 'for a girl who committed suicide.'

'How can we find out anything about any of them?' asked Sheila.

'Oh, by just looking around,' said Dawlish, vaguely. 'Felicity will probably have some ideas. You won't make it obvious, of course.'

'We'll see what we can do,' said Felicity, and added pertinently: 'Why are you interested in Calshott, Pat?'

'Curiosity,' Dawlish said at last. 'Item 1, a milk lorry belonging to the S.W.W.D.C., item 2, a possibly murdered girl working at ditto, item 3, a doctor named Brett who once worked at ditto as the factory doctor but retired soon afterwards and lived a life of ease.'

Felicity's eyes widened. 'Did Brett work for the Company?'

'Yes. Moreover, Bligh knows it but didn't say so willingly. He must know it, he must have seen the connection and should be making inquiries. If he is, he hasn't told me. If he isn't he must have a good reason, for he's not a fool and he wouldn't miss the fact that the S.W.W.D.C. keeps butting into this affair.'

'Have the police examined the stuff from the syringe?' Sheila asked.

'Not yet, but they're about to do so. They've tested the powder in your pit, Sheila—it's lime. Ordinary garden agricultural lime. If anyone can tell me why they dug a pit and gave it a cement floor and then stored lime in it, it would be a big help.'

At half past four Dawlish went downstairs to see whether Corbett had arrived. A few minute's later he came up on a bicycle. He looked fit enough and there was nothing to suggest the physical weakness which Bligh had explained so fully. *Too* fully, Dawlish wondered?

'What are we going to do?' Corbett asked.

'Could we have tea at your place?' asked Dawlish, 'and work the situation out there? I've a talk with Dickerson in mind, of course—if he's still in the ditch.'

'He was half an hour ago,' said Corbett, a little sheepishly. 'I gave him a drink of water.'

Dawlish frowned. 'A pity,' he said, 'the less he gets in the way of sympathy the more easily he'll talk—but a sip of water won't make much difference, I suppose.'

He drove to the cottage, after they had tied Corbett's cycle on the back of the M.G. Corbett made some tea and cut some bread-and-butter which they ate while standing up in the kitchen.

Soon afterwards, they went to see Dickerson, who under questioning still maintained a sullen silence. That the man was frightened went without saying, but Dawlish could not rid himself of a feeling that he was equally frightened of someone— or something—else.

Dawlish decided to let him wait a little longer before really trying to break down his resistance. In the meantime he would get what information he could from a search of Wood Grange.

There was no sign of anyone in the grounds of Wood Grange; but beyond the brick wall were several policemen and members of the unit whose tank had been sent over the hill. Dawlish had been told by Bligh that the tank had come to rest harmlessly on the rocks near the river and that no one had been injured; the only fatality on that grim day had been the nurse.

No one answered the knocking and ringing at the door.

Dawlish and Corbett walked round to the back of the house but found everything securely locked, even the garage and the garden shed. There was no sign of the gardener.

'Birds flown,' murmured Dawlish. 'Do you feel energetic?'

'In what way?' asked Corbett.

'The windows are a bit narrow for me,' said Dawlish.

'You mean you're prepared to—' Corbett paused, then grinned and nodded. Dawlish, who had seen a small window unlatched, opened it wider and held it open while Corbett climbed through. It was near the kitchen door, which he opened after a very few seconds.

There was no one in the downstair rooms, but in the kitchen quarters it looked as if the servants had packed hastily. There were pieces of string and packing paper on the table and other signs of hurried departure. Except for one room upstairs, all the doors were unlocked. The beds were made and the rooms tidy. Dawlish spent five minutes packing Sheila's clothes, then looked on the second floor, reserved for the servants. Here, too, there were signs of hasty departure.

'It's a curious business,' Corbett said, looking round him.

'I don't trust appearances,' answered Dawlish.

He was very much on the *qui vive*; when he opened doors he did so cautiously, his right hand in his coat pocket holding a gun.

At last they finished the search except for the one locked room—Dickerson's study. The silence was disturbing, and neither of them felt at ease.

Dawlish took out a key-case, selected a long, thin skeleton key, looking at Corbett with a smile.

'This is all strictly illegal,' he said, 'but the police will probably wink at it.' He inserted the key in the lock and played it about, until, after a very short while, the lock clicked back and, when Dawlish turned the handle, the door opened.

'Hurry up!' urged Corbett.

'No need for hurry,' said Dawlish. 'Move to one side, old man.' He kept his fingers on the handle waiting for Corbett to obey, and then, stepping to the other side of the door himself, pushed it wider open.

Something fell.

Dawlish swung round shouting a warning. Both men went down on their faces. The 'something' struck the carpet with a dull thud and then exploded. The ensuing roar deafened them but did not rob Dawlish of his senses. A flash of light forced itself against his eyes, he heard the thudding of pieces of wood and plaster and brick against the opposite wall. Dawlish, already stumbling to his feet wondered if the incendiary bomb—for such it was—had been put there to catch him or whether there was anything in the room that Dickerson wanted destroyed before a search could be made.

He went quickly to Corbett's aid; helped him to his feet, and told him sharply to keep well back. The younger man appeared stunned, his face a deathly white, but otherwise unhurt.

The carpet was burning fiercely and flames were running wildly about, setting fire to everything they touched. The doorway was well alight, but only up to a height of his knees; Dawlish stepped quickly through the flames and into the room.

He had no time to look about him before he saw the body of a man, huddled over the desk. He had no difficulty in recognising it to be that of Dr. Brett.

CHAPTER SIXTEEN

DOWN ON THE FARM

When Dawlish reached Brett the fire was gaining a fiercer hold behind him and he knew that if he were to prevent it spreading he would have to act quickly. He felt Brett's pulse, and detected movement. The man was breathing, despite an ugly knife wound in his neck. Dawlish, casting ideas of fire-fighting aside, stepped to the window and thrust it open.

There was ample foothold and had it been a matter of his own escape alone it would have been easy. The difficulty was to get Brett out. Gently, Dawlish hoisted the man over his shoulder. Smoke and the stench of the burning carpet were acrid in his nostrils, while the heat was almost unbearable.

Cautiously, he began to climb out of the window.

Another sharp explosion inside the room flung a piece of molten fire against Brett's shoulder. It flared up close to Dawlish's face. Dawlish shifted the man's weight, and, using the sleeve of his coat, brushed the blazing fragment away.

Inside, the room was a raging inferno and he knew that even had he stayed to try to fight the flames he would have failed.

He reached downwards, sought and found a foothold. Still keeping a hand on the sill he considered the possibility of jumping down, but was afraid that if he did so Brett might slip; and the jolt kill him. His ears filled with the roar of flames, he did not think of help coming from outside until he distinguished the sound of voices.

Something loomed up at his side; with a rush of relief he recognised the top rung of a ladder.

Once on it, he went down quickly. Before he reached the ground men were reaching up to take Brett's body from his shoulders. Some were in uniform, others were country-folk—and among them was Corbett, who, it proved, had shouted for help and attracted the attention of the men searching the grounds outside the house.

Stretching his agonised limbs after the strain, Dawlish looked dispassionately at Brett, now lying unconscious on the ground.

'I've 'phoned for an ambulance and the fire brigade,' Corbett said, quickly.

'Good man. What is the chance of getting on top of that little blaze, I wonder?'

'Not much,' said Corbett.

It was only too obvious that he was right. Although men were hurrying to and from Wood Grange bringing out what furniture they could lay their hands on, the whole house was now ablaze. Soon an inside wall collapsed with a rumbling crash. There followed a period of quiet, broken only by the roar of the flames, some of which were shooting out from windows and doors. In the middle of the strange lull the clear ringing of the fire-engine bell came from the road.

'That frees us,' Dawlish said to Corbett.

Soon afterwards Bligh arrived. Dawlish exchanged a few

words with him, gave him a brief outline of what had happened, then walked slowly away from the blazing house.

'They've made sure we don't find anything there,' Corbett said, with a touch of bitterness.

'They've made sure that the credulous among us think it was worth destroying,' Dawlish said drily.

'What do you mean?' demanded Corbett.

'Wood Grange was the seat of the trouble, Wood Grange is burning down,' intoned Dawlish. 'Therefore, no seat; if no seat, no trouble!' He laid a hand on Corbett's shoulder. 'Mind if we go to your farm?'

Dawlish drove steadily to Grange Farm. He had to pass Corbett's cottage, but vetoed another visit to Dickerson.

The farm stood back from the road. Built of stone, the garden bright with flowers, it was a charming sight. Little more than a mile from the burning house, it might have been in a different world.

'I wish I knew why you'd come here,' Corbett said.

Dawlish stopped the M.G. and climbed out, slowly.

'Well,' he pointed out, 'there is much roguery afoot, you know, and it's happening near here. Wood Grange has gone, but because the seat of the trouble is no more, it doesn't mean that we've nothing else to worry about. It would be very helpful if I could make arrangement with Simpson, who you say is an obliging sort of fellow, to let me prowl around from time to time without having to explain myself.'

They approached the farmhouse leisurely. Dawlish saw that there were shutters at the windows, and as he waited for the door to be opened he played idly with one of them, surprised to find how heavy it was. He was eyeing it curiously when Corbett, who had gone round the back way, opened the front door.

'Pretty weighty, isn't it?' Dawlish asked, idly.

'It's blast-proof, or supposed to be,' said Corbett, 'all the windows and doors are fitted like that, Mrs. Simpson is nervous of bombing.'

They found the farmer in his office. Dawlish had expected a burly, rough-clad countryman, but found a grey-haired man of some culture and steadiness of eye. He regarded Dawlish expectantly, his expression questioning.

Dawlish smiled amiably.

'Good of you to allow Corbett to give me a hand, Mr. Simpson, and I hope you won't regret it.'

'Why should I?' asked Simpson.

'Because it's encouraged me to worry you for more,' said Dawlish. 'I would be exceedingly grateful if you would allow me to look round from time to time.'

'Why should you want to do that?'

Dawlish shrugged. 'Whatever is happening has its centre about here.' He went on to ask whether he could rent a room at the farm, pointing out that there might be some degree of danger and explaining that he was very interested in *l'affaire* Dickerson and hoped to see it through to the end. Simpson considered the proposition at some length.

At last he said:

'Exactly why do you want a room, Mr. Dawlish?'

'Perhaps to sleep, perhaps to eat, perhaps to sit and think,' said Dawlish.

'For no illegal purpose?' Simpson asked.

'My dear sir, no!'

He fancied that there was a faint smile in the farmer's eyes.

'I'm glad to have that assurance,' he said drily, 'because your reputation has reached Terne, Major Dawlish. Mind you, I'm not saying that I don't think you're wasting your time in coming here, but if you want a room I've no doubt it can be arranged.'

'That's very good of you.'

'My wife will be back on the five-thirty bus,' the farmer continued, 'and she'll show it to you.' He picked up a smooth-bowled pipe from his desk. 'I have heard,' he went on, 'that Dickerson is missing.' He looked mildly curious.

'He certainly doesn't seem to be about,' Dawlish admitted. 'You don't like him, I gather?'

'I do not,' said Simpson, and left it at that.

'Oh, by the way'—Dawlish spoke casually—'do you send your milk to the West Country Wholesale Dairy?'

'As a matter of fact, I do.'

'A good firm?' asked Dawlish, noting Corbett's restless movements.

'Excellent, and not taken over body and soul by the Milk Marketing Board, I'm glad to say! There can be too much Government control.'

'There can, indeed! You have lorries here once a day?'

'Twice,' Simpson corrected him, as Corbett broke in:

'Where is all this leading to, Dawlish?'

'Probably nowhere,' said Dawlish, blandly, 'but I'm interested in one of the drivers. A little fellow I think, with a snub nose.'

Simpson frowned and pushed his chair back, his voice, when he spoke, came harshly.

'I would like to know exactly why you are interested in him, Major Dawlish?'

'Passing interest only,' Dawlish said.

'The man was involved in a serious accident not long after leaving here,' said Simpson. 'He was killed on the other side of Terne.'

'Well, well,' said Dawlish, after a pause. 'So they killed him to make sure that he couldn't talk. As they tried to kill Brett.' He stood up quickly. 'I don't like it,' he said. 'I'll be back—can you come, Corbett?'

Simpson nodded permission to Corbett.

'Too many deaths—far too many,' Dawlish said, as he started the M.G. 'It looks as if panic has set in, and frightened people do peculiar things. Ah!' They came in sight of the cottage and he pulled up with a squeal of brakes, leapt out and hurried past the cottage towards the copse, the tank trap, and Dickerson. Corbett followed him.

'Are you going to tackle Dickerson now?'

'I think we might,' said Dawlish, slowly. 'I certainly think we might.'

They were twenty yards from the man, who was half-buried by the long grass growing from the foot and the sides of the tank trap, when Dawlish suddenly quickened his pace.

'What is it?' Corbett asked anxiously.

'Shoes,' said Dawlish in a wondering voice. 'We took them off.' He reached Dickerson and stood peering down at his legs which terminated in a pair of polished oxfords.

'Great Scott!' gasped Corbett. 'It's not—'

His voice trailed off as Dawlish went down on one knee, raised the man from the ditch, took the gag from his mouth and heard a croaking voice say something which was quite incoherent. It was obvious that it was not Dickerson.

'Well, well,' said Dawlish, for once at a loss. 'So we have been foxed. Recognise him?'

Corbett drew a deep breath.

'Yes,' he said, and paused. 'Yes, it's—Mr. Waring.'

'Oh,' said Dawlish, raising the man and cutting the cords at wrists and ankles. 'Mind telling me who the devil Waring *is*?'

'He's the manager of the Wholesale Dairy Company,' Corbett said in a strangled voice. 'Dawlish, what do you know?'

CHAPTER SEVENTEEN

RESULTS OF SOME INQUIRIES

'Nothing,' said Dawlish cheerfully, as he helped the other to his feet. 'Is that better, sir?' Waring stood swaying, moving his mouth in grotesque fashion and obviously trying to speak. 'Lend me a hand, Corbett.' Together they helped the manager of the Dairy Company out of the ditch; once on level ground he was able to walk, although they had to support him.

They reached the cottage and Dawlish lowered the man into an easy chair, while Corbett went to get water and a towel.

In ten minutes or so the manager was sipping a cup of tea, held in both rather shaky hands. He drew a deep breath. 'I thought no one would ever find me!'

Dawlish said gently: 'Who put you there?'

'I don't know.'

Dawlish hid his disappointment. 'Were you just grabbed out of the air, so to speak, and dumped down?'

'I was on my way to see Simpson,' Waring said. 'Do you know him?'

'Assume that I do,' said Dawlish, 'and that I now stand in the place of a policeman.' He smiled, but his eyes were sombre.

'So you were on your way to see Simpson, about—' he paused hopefully.

'There has been a shortage of milk in some of his churns,' Waring said, eyeing Dawlish curiously. 'Who *are* you?'

'Dawlish is the name,' said the large man.

It would not have been surprising had Waring shown a blank non-recognition. Instead, had Dawlish announced himself to be Queen of the May Waring could not have been more surprised.

'Heard of me?' Dawlish inquired.

'Er—yes.' Waring was obviously trying to pull himself together. 'Your name has been bandied about the town for the past few hours,' he said, 'and there are some surprising stories about you.'

Dawlish chuckled. 'I've no doubt you could cut it by half,' he said, 'but don't let it spoil your story.'

It appeared that Waring had been driving towards Grange Farm just after three o'clock and, at the top of the hill, two men had thumbed him for a lift. He had told them he was going only half a mile farther on, but before he had finished speaking, one man had pulled a gun, the other had dragged him from his seat. He had been knocked unconscious and woken up in the ditch, gagged and bound. Beyond that, Waring said, he knew nothing.

'Who knew where you were going?' Dawlish asked.

'Two or three of my staff knew, but I don't see that that has anything to do with what happened to me.'

'It could have. They knew why you were going, of course?'

'Yes,' said Waring, 'but—'

'Did you know about this milk shortage?' Dawlish asked Corbett.

'It's news to me,' said Corbett. 'We're always very careful to make sure that the churns are full. Simpson is too conscientious, if anything.'

'That is why I came out to see him myself,' said Waring. 'When I telephoned him and he assured me that there was no shortage when the milk left the farm, I decided to visit him personally.'

'Hum,' said Dawlish. 'How much shortage, Mr. Waring?'

'Two or three churns have been half-empty,' said Waring.

'H'm. Pilfering for the black market?'

'That's what I feared.'

'Who could it be?'

Waring paused. 'I don't like making guesses,' he said at last, 'but as far as I can see it was either someone at the farm, which I can't believe, or my lorry driver—which is equally unbelievable.'

Dawlish said: 'When did you leave your office?'

'Oh, quite early this morning—I have been out most of the day.'

'So you don't know about the lorry that crashed and the driver who died,' murmured Dawlish. 'Was it always the same driver who took the lorry to Grange Farm?'

'Yes. *What* did you say?'

Dawlish told him, and saw that the man was genuinely upset. It transpired that he was already troubled by the 'suicide' of the girl who had defaulted in the Accounts Department. Obviously Waring was trying to keep a hold on himself yet found the circumstances too much for him. Corbett also seemed bewildered.

Dawlish suggested that Corbett should return to the farm while he took Waring back to Terne.

It was a silent drive, for Waring was deep in thought and Dawlish equally absorbed.

He was quite sure that he had been watched from the copse, that Dickerson's friends had known where the man was and had deliberately left him for a while, to lull Dawlish into a false sense of security. The ruse had succeeded, and it did not please him.

He dropped Waring outside the offices of the S.W.W.D.C., then turned and drove to the *George*. He hoped that Felicity and Sheila would be back, but they were not. He dropped into the easy chair, tired and more than a little worried. The truth, as Dawlish saw it, was that he had succeeded in his first objective of forcing the 'other side' to take evasive action, but that they had done so with more success than he had either anticipated or wanted.

He telephoned Bligh, who told him that Brett was still unconscious and on the danger list, that Wood Grange had been completely destroyed, and that he would like to see him later in the evening.

'Always at your service,' said Dawlish, heartily. Going up to the room again, he tried to see through the confusion which he himself had largely created. He had come to make general inquiries, had succeeded in prodding the unknown people who backed Dickerson and Brett into greater violence than was their wont. He regretted the absence of his friends; for one thing, he would have liked Corbett followed. Uneasily, he admitted the possibility that Corbett had disclosed Dickerson's whereabouts.

The man might be playing a very clever double game, but— *what* game?

Lime pits dug in the hill, mysterious disappearances, the death of a girl—he was convinced that the girl had not committed suicide but been murdered—as also had been the lorry driver. (The death of the nurse had been accidental; it had occurred because the sharpshooters had wanted to kill Sheila before she could talk of the pit—or, possibly, because they thought she might have seen the men who had pulled her out of it.) The sharpshooters themselves had come well into the open, disclosing something of the strength of their organisation. That

Dickerson and Brett were men of some consequence in it, was obvious.

The lime pits, then, and the murders—he believed that the latter had been committed to silence people who might have talked dangerously—and, a shortage of milk in the churns from Grange Farm. That had something to do with the general scheme, he was sure.

One thing's certain, he thought. Bligh will have to get busy on the Dairy Company. He wondered if he should go and telephone Bligh again, then heard voices in the passage, Felicity's and Sheila's.

When the two girls entered, it was obvious that they were on the tip-toe of excitement.

'Pat!' cried Felicity, closing the door quickly, 'I think we've found something that will really help!'

'Dickerson!' exclaimed Sheila.

'Dickerson or his double,' said Felicity.

'Go on,' said Dawlish, gently.

'He's—*if* it is Dickerson—he arrived at the milk company office about half-past four,' said Felicity. 'We were making inquiries about Mildred Gay—pretending to be reporters—when he came in by a side door. He hurried up the stairs and stayed there, until Sir Mortimer Calshott came.'

'*Who?*'

'Sir Mortimer Calshott.'

'Well, well,' murmured Dawlish. 'And you left them there together? Were the police about?'

'Some were,' said Felicity. 'Pat, there's another thing. Mildred Gay's fiancé worked for the company and was killed when a lorry crashed this afternoon.'

Dawlish said, softly: 'Her fiancé, was he? Shall we come back to that later? What about Dickerson and Calshott?'

'We didn't leave until *they* left, in Calshott's car,' said Felicity quickly. 'Dickerson had shaved off his beard and moustache, and I couldn't *swear* that it was Dickerson.'

'Oh, it *was*,' said Sheila. 'That is, if it could have been.' She eyed Dawlish hopefully.

'It could have been,' Dawlish assured her. 'A different suit and no beard—enough to escape recognition at a casual glance. You don't know where they went?'

'Only that they were in a Rolls-Royce with a chauffeur,' Felicity said.

'*Calshott* can't disappear into thin air,' said Sheila.

'Can't he?' asked Dawlish, moving swiftly towards the door. 'I hope you're right. I won't be long.' He opened the door and stepped out—and as he did so someone fired at him from along the passage.

There was no attempt to keep the shooting secret, the roar of the shot echoed about the hotel and Dawlish fell flat on his face, in a single movement; the bullet tore through the padding of his shoulder and he heard it thud into the wall near him. A second shot made more noise than the first.

Dawlish rolled over on his back and then sprang to his feet. He saw a man's hat outlined against an open window at the far end of the passage, heard someone shouting. He wrenched his gun from his pocket and sprinted along the passage; but by the time he reached the window, the wearer of the hat was running across the courtyard of the *George* towards a motorcycle.

Corbett was approaching from the street.

The wearer of the hat stopped and raised his gun. Had he fired at such point-blank range, Corbett would have stood no earthly chance. Instead, Dawlish fired from the window. He did no more than take the man's hat from his head, but it gave Corbett the time to rush into the attack. Dawlish's second shot punctured the front tyre of the motor-cycle.

'What the devil's happening?' demanded an irate voice.

Dawlish, already beginning to climb out of the window to go to Corbett's help, recognised the voice as Bligh's. He grinned and waved the hand which held the gun, before dropping from the window to the cobbles below.

As he picked himself up and turned to the fray he saw Corbett falling from a punch which seemed first to lift him off the ground. The gunman leapt on his motor-cycle, but the flat tyre made it almost impossible for the machine to start. He looked over his shoulder despairingly—and in that moment Dawlish recognised the murderer of the Red Cross nurse.

'Enough is enough,' said Dawlish, gently.

The other made no reply, but levelled his automatic. Dawlish's blow sent the gun flying. The man sprawled to the ground, the motor-cycle on top of him.

By then the courtyard was filled with excited people and Dawlish's wish to interrogate the man without police or witnesses, became as useless as wishing for the moon.

Then he stared, for in the forefront of the crowd he recognised Dippy Fowler of the *Sunday Cry*.

He sauntered up, with a lop-sided grin. ''Lo, Dawlish. Luck meeting you. You're always good for a story.'

'You're always good at embellishing one,' Dawlish answered repressively, 'but I shouldn't write this up yet, if I were you.'

'I might do a deal,' Fowler said, as indifferent as Dawlish to the people surrounding him. 'I want a word with you, Dawlish— you'll be glad to hear what I've got to say.'

'Later,' said Dawlish.

Fowler answered imperturbably. 'Now or never, I'm in a hurry.'

Before Dawlish had time to consider this, Bligh arrived. 'One prisoner,' Dawlish told him, 'and we might be able to get something out of him if we try hard enough. Meanwhile, a word in your ear.' He leaned forward and whispered: 'Can you put a call out for Calshott in his Rolls-Royce—he has Dickerson with him.'

'Oh,' said Bligh. His stolid face gave nothing away, but Dawlish liked neither his manner nor the way he uttered the word. 'No,' went on Bligh. 'I can't, Dawlish, and in any case there isn't any need, he's at my office now. He's waiting to see you, and so is Dickerson. I'm afraid, this time, you've gone rather too far.'

The large man stared at him blankly.

'Too far? What are you—'

He paused. Behind Bligh, he could see Fowler nodding his head towards the drive-in of the *George*. The man was swiftly lost in the crowd, while Bligh continued to stare at Dawlish with more than a touch of hostility.

'Brett's dead,' he said, 'but before he died he told us that it was you who attacked him. Dickerson's reported the same thing.' Bligh was absurdly formal. 'As for Sir Mortimer, as our Chief Constable he thinks something should be done about it.'

CHAPTER EIGHTEEN

DAWLISH GETS THE BIT IN HIS TEETH

Dawlish resisted a temptation to push the policeman aside and to follow Dippy Fowler. As Felicity had crowded up behind Bligh, Dawlish muttered a quick aside.

'Find Dippy Fowler, Fel, he's in the town. Learn what he has to say.'

'What's that?' asked Bligh, suspiciously.

'A greeting to my wife,' said Dawlish blandly. 'All right, Bligh, I'll come quietly. You'll spare a moment to find out why this little customer shot at me, won't you?'

'Naturally,' Bligh said.

'Surely—' began Sheila.

'Keep your eye on Corbett for me,' said Dawlish with a wink, 'I think he could do with some gentle ministrations.'

A dozen or so people followed Dawlish and Bligh along the High Street, while others fell in behind. Dawlish was satisfied enough at Bligh's silence. He wished to think.

The speed of events since Felicity had told him of Dickerson's visit to the Dairy Company had allowed little time for anything but action. It seemed only a few seconds since he had suggested Bligh should put out a call for Sir Mortimer Calshott. He was more amused than annoyed by his own ignorance of Calshott's other position; that the man was the Chief Constable of Dayshire seemed to Dawlish to explain a great many things. He hummed to himself. Bligh looked at him curiously.

'You don't seem perturbed,' he said.

'Who, me?' asked Dawlish, surprised. 'That will be the day. But I think I could name some people who are,' he added brightly.

Bligh said nothing, but waited for him to go up the steps of the police station first. Dawlish was convinced that the man expected him to make a dash for safety.

Once he turned, as at a sudden thought.

'Why didn't you tell me that Calshott was the Chief Constable, Bligh?'

'I assumed that you knew,' said Bligh.

'Oh, no,' said Dawlish, 'I don't think that was the reason.' He shook his head as one humouring a wayward child. 'Aren't you going to tell me what Calshott wants and what your earlier, rather cryptic utterances mean?'

'I think I've said enough,' Bligh told him.

'We-ell, perhaps,' conceded Dawlish. 'Brett has accused me of attacking him, yes? Dickerson ditto. Yes?'

'This is the room,' said Bligh. He tapped at the door, opened it, and stood aside for Dawlish to pass. Dawlish stepped into the room, lifting a hand in greeting. He was not surprised to see Dickerson sitting there. Though shorn of his beard, he was perfectly recognisable.

Sir Mortimer Calshott sat behind a desk.

'Calshott?' murmured Dawlish. 'Very glad to see you, I've been looking for you for some time!' Plump and well-dressed,

Dawlish could see he was no fool. 'Dickerson's been romancing a little, I understand,' he went on.

Dickerson did not rise to the bait, but Calshott raised a hand for silence and, in the same movement, motioned to a chair.

'This is a remarkable case and I have decided to interview you myself, Major Dawlish. Please sit down.'

'I'm afraid I can't,' said Dawlish. 'Someone kicked me.' He rubbed the side of his leg tenderly. 'Hobnailed boot, too.'

'If you insist on pretending to be so obtuse, I cannot help it,' said Calshott. 'I may say, Dawlish, that but for the fact that I understand you were asked to come here by no less a person than a Superintendent of Scotland Yard I would not behave in this way.'

'Well, well, you mean that you are being particularly lenient? May I mention—in the least crude way possible, that I, too, have friends in high places? Dickerson isn't the only chappie who can go over the heads of the ordinary policeman. May I also mention, for fuller measure, that I am an Intelligence Officer. Not on duty, it's true, but don't, please, think that Dickerson's word will necessarily be taken against mine.'

Calshott flushed. 'If you are implying—'

'Not implying, stating,' said Dawlish. 'Dickerson told you that I broke into his house, assaulting him and his friends, making up fantastic stories about poisonous injections.'

'I—' began Calshott.

'Please,' interrupted Dawlish quietly, 'allow me to continue. After abducting Dickerson, leaving him bound and gagged, in a ditch, I then returned to Wood Grange, attacked and murdered Dr. Brett, set the house on fire—all on the pretence that it was for the sake of law and order, but actually to grab the gems. Is that not so?'

'You can't deny—' began Dickerson.

'Oh, but I am denying,' said Dawlish, 'and flatly. Of course,

I might add, for effect, that I waited in the house long enough to pull Brett out of the window, but Dickerson would doubtless say that I wanted it to appear as if I had risked my life to save him. Evidence by contradiction, in other words—didn't he say just that?'

'I think I have heard enough from you,' said Calshott, sharply.

'Not quite,' said Dawlish. 'My innings, since Dickerson has had his. People have died, you know, in this little set-up. Several people. A milk lorry driver, a girl from the milk company's office, housekeepers, a Red Cross nurse. There may be others, I'm afraid. Some of the bodies, buried in pits and covered with lime, and a dressing of earth and scrub put over them—hard to find, but they will be found and contrary to popular belief lime doesn't devour the *corpus* as quickly as all that. The murderers must have discovered this, for the one girl was drowned and the driver killed in a clumsy accident. The driver because he knew why the milk from Grange Farm was short, the girl in the Accounts Department because she also discovered why. Did you know that the girl who died and the lorry driver who died were engaged to be married? Interesting fact. Girl is drowned, lorry driver is scared, told to act on instructions or he'll die too. Poor spirit, but he obeyed and was ready to smash into me, my wife, M.G. and all, and swear that it was all a ghastly accident. Nicely planned, wasn't it?' Dawlish spoke too swiftly for the others to have an opportunity for interrupting, and when he paused to smile at Dickerson, who had gone pale and was sitting very upright in his chair, none of them appeared to want to speak—Calshott looked completely taken aback. '*Very* nicely planned,' continued Dawlish. 'Also Brett, getting frightened, had to be killed. Very neat touch to murder him, although it didn't quite work. Very loyal, Brett. Probably thought I *did* attack him, and what greater proof could you have than the word of a murdered man?'

Dickerson snapped: 'Have we got to listen to this?'

'Oh, there's more,' said Dawlish laconically. 'I haven't finished by a long way. Situation was working out, but Bligh didn't like it. It worried him because it so obviously affected *your* company, Calshott, so he had a word with the Yard. Yard made tentative inquiries, saw the delicacy of the situation, and selected me to be the cat's paw. I can almost hear Trivett saying: "If there's anything there, Dawlish will blunder into it"—That's the worst of having a reputation!' He looked at Bligh, standing very stiffly by the window.

Calshott said, quietly:

'Is this true, Bligh? Did you approach Scotland Yard?'

'No, sir,' said Bligh. 'I discussed it with a friend of mine from the Yard, who happened to be in Terne on holiday.'

'Happened to be!' echoed Dawlish. '*Such* irreproachable behaviour on Bligh's part, and the blame for this unwarrantable interference in a purely local business is that of the Yard's. Well, it serves, and the Yard has broad shoulders. The thing is, we now know the position. Bligh stymied, couldn't suspect his own Chief, the Yard couldn't take official action without being formally approached—but I needn't go into that again, need I? What matters is that I saw the way the wind was blowing when I left here earlier in the afternoon and I telephoned the Yard. Dirty work, I said, I'm about to be framed. If I know William Trivett, he's half-way here by now.' Dawlish delivered this mendacious statement with great gusto. 'If you detain me against the advice of a senior officer from Scotland Yard, Calshott, people will begin to wonder things. A rather uncomfortable state for those concerned.'

'The man is a born liar,' said Dickerson, thinly.

Dawlish laughed. 'Worried, Dickerson? No protection from the Chief Constable after all?'

Calshott said stiffly:

'I hope you are aware that you are making one slanderous statement after another.'

'Oh, no,' said Dawlish. 'I'm acquainted with the law of slander. Also, some of the elementary rules of the criminal code. Thus, sir, when I lay a charge against a man of aiding and abetting murder, that charge is investigated, and a man under such a charge is automatically suspended from any position connected with the police.'

Calshott stared at him. 'What do you mean?'

'Guess,' said Dawlish, blandly, and turned to Dickerson. 'The best thing you can do is to make a clean breast of it. You won't stand an earthly unless you do, but there is such a thing as King's Evidence.'

None of the others spoke.

'All tongue-tied?' asked Dawlish. 'My fault, I'm afraid. Why don't you admit, Dickerson, that you have deliberately attracted attention, deliberately accepted the blame for many things which have happened, almost certainly under compulsion? After all, compulsion would be a good plea. You hired the housekeepers, someone else disposed of them. You might even get lenient treatment by proving that you didn't know what was going to happen to them.'

'I have done nothing—' began Dickerson in a thin voice, only to break off when Calshott pushed his chair back and stared at Dawlish. Being no higher than Dawlish's chin, he did not look as impressive as he doubtless intended, but he had a measure of dignity as he asked:

'Can you substantiate any of your accusations against Mr. Dickerson?'

Dawlish raised an eyebrow. 'In time, I can.'

He admitted to himself that he had reached the limit of plausible mendacity. That he had caused a certain consternation gave him some satisfaction, but would it prove enough? A gentle perspiration covered his forehead, although he smiled into the Chief Constable's eyes. When all was said and done, even the Chief Constable of an obscure county had some authority; the Yard's might not be strong enough to break it, certainly could not without sufficient evidence. Ideas were not evidence.

He had never wished so heartily for the sight of Bill Trivett's face, nor wished a lie the truth. If only he had adopted Felicity's suggestion earlier!

The telephone on Calshott's desk rang.

Calshott, obviously about to deliver himself of a weighty pronouncement, turned irritably to Bligh.

'See who that is,' he said. 'Say that I am engaged, unless it has to do with this case.'

'Yes, sir.' Bligh stepped forward and lifted the receiver. 'This is the office of the Chief Constable,' he said. 'Yes . . . *Who*? . . . Er—yes, hold on a moment.' He put his left hand over the mouthpiece, his face blank with surprise and chagrin. 'It—er—it's Superintendent Trivett of Scotland Yard, sir, downstairs, asking for you.'

CHAPTER NINETEEN

UNEASY PEACE

Happily, Calshott and Dickerson were staring at Bligh, for neither could have been as startled as Dawlish.

At last Bligh broke a prolonged silence.

'Will you see him, sir?'

'Yes,' Calshott said sharply, 'have him sent up.' He looked at Dawlish. 'So you had the impertinence to get in touch with Scotland Yard, Dawlish, without first consulting me.'

'Trivett's a friend of mine,' said Dawlish, amiably. 'We seem to have a lot of mutual friends at the Yard, don't we?'

Calshott deliberated, twisting a pencil in his fingers, then looked at Dickerson.

'Is there anything more you wish to say?'

'I hope I don't need to say any more,' said Dickerson, in a strangled voice. 'I have told you that Dawlish murdered Dr. Brett and I insist—'

'I shall be glad if you will wait downstairs,' said Calshott, his voice completely expressionless. 'Send for a man, Bligh, to escort Mr. Dickerson to the waiting room.'

Dickerson said: 'I am in a hurry, I have—'

'I hope that it will not be necessary to keep you long,' said Calshott.

A sergeant arrived and Dickerson was leaving the room, obviously taken by surprise at the change in Calshott's manner, when Trivett appeared, preceded by a constable. His glance swept quickly over Dickerson, then he smiled at Dawlish. Calshott rounded his desk but did not immediately speak.

'Allow me to present—' began Dawlish, and after he had introduced Trivett, added: 'I'm very glad you took me seriously, Bill, I hoped you'd come down.'

'Felicity told me it was urgent,' said Trivett.

'Felicity?'—Dawlish began. 'Bless her heart!' He had decided against ringing London, but Felicity had apparently taken it into her own hands. 'Have you seen her?' he asked.

Trivett nodded; there was a faint smile in his eyes, suggesting that he had weighed up the situation and knew what manner of spot Dawlish was in. True, he could not know that Dawlish had spent the last twenty minutes antagonising the Chief Constable, but that faded into the background as Calshott, very stiff and formal, asked Trivett whether he were in Terne officially and, if so, on what authority.

'On Home Office authority, sir.'

'Better and better,' crowed Dawlish to himself, as Trivett produced a document from his pocket, unfolded it and handed it to Calshott, who read it with compressed lips.

'Thank you, Superintendent. I am asked to give you all the assistance in my power—I will, of course, I am at your service.'

'It would be a help,' Dawlish said irrepressibly, 'if you could convince the Chief Constable that I'm not likely to be a murderer, Bill. My fault, I suppose, as I've been rather free with innuendo.' He smiled, unrepentantly. 'Apologies are due, I'm afraid.'

Calshott stared at him.

'What exactly do you mean?'

'I am apologising as handsomely as I can for suggesting that you were a king-pin in this sad business,' Dawlish said, glibly. 'After all, Dickerson was relying on your sense of fairness and his built-up case about the murder of Brett. Having got your ear he might have expected to keep it. So by telling him that I had tried to start a revolt in Terne and by throwing out hints that you were liable to be removed I disturbed his confidence. Disturbed confidence is the first thing in the downfall of dictators and malefactors, don't you think?'

Trivett allowed himself a brief smile.

'What has Dawlish been up to, sir? I'm afraid, unless you're used to him, you may find his methods a little unorthodox.'

'You're right there,' said Calshott, heavily. 'Do you mean to tell me, Dawlish, that you talked as you did solely to upset Dickerson?'

'Well, I didn't do it just to upset you,' said Dawlish. 'If I did so, it was merely an unfortunate incidental. The thing is, Bill—'

He went through much that he had said, occasionally dropping in suggestions that he knew how badly Sir Mortimer must have felt about it and how much he regretted that but—warming to his task—emphasised the need for completely upsetting Dickerson's hopes and plans. Much of it was unconvincing but all of it was plausible. As he finished Dawlish was relieved to see a faint smile in Calshott's eyes and to see that Bligh was smiling. Only Trivett frowned, as he burst out explosively:

'Confound you, Pat, you should guard that tongue of yours!'

'I plead extreme provocation,' said Dawlish hastily. 'After all, I had just been shot at. Besides, I was accused of killing Brett when I had nearly killed myself trying to keep him alive. Not soothing, was it?'

Trivett lifted his hands helplessly.

'I'm afraid it's as much my fault as anyone's, sir, for wishing Dawlish on to you. But'—he frowned—'this allegation on Brett's part is serious. Did he actually name Dawlish as his assailant?'

Bligh said quickly: 'His actual words, as taken down by the sergeant who was with him when he said it, were "*This is Dawlish's work, he's arranged it*".'

Dawlish stared at Calshott.

'Well, well. No direct accusation there.'

'It *could* be taken two ways,' Trivett said thoughtfully.

'Dickerson also made the accusation,' Calshott said.

'But then, Dickerson is a liar,' said Dawlish, blandly.

'Possibly, but such an accusation has to be investigated.'

'I was coming to that,' said Dawlish. 'I had been with Corbett most of the hour or two preceding the discovery of Brett's misadventure. Less than half an hour before I had been at Grange Farm, where Mr. Simpson saw me. Corbett and I then found a Mr. Waring—' he paused.

'Waring?' asked Calshott, quickly.

'Your manager,' said Dawlish. 'He had been waylaid and bound and placed in the ditch. He will tell you something of what happened and bear out part of my story. For the rest, Corbett was with me when I found Brett and he will tell you that an explosive incendiary placed to go off as the door opened, nearly made the discovery of Brett impossible. Brett was bleeding freely when I found him, medical evidence will tell you that he had been knifed perhaps half an hour before the commotion at Wood Grange, when I was with Corbett.' His eyebrows rose. 'I hope that lets me out.'

'Why didn't you say this before?' asked Calshott.

'Why should I tell Dickerson everything?' Dawlish answered. 'Besides, I thought it might be a good idea if Dickerson believed me to be under arrest. Don't think me swollen-headed, but I have a feeling that he would like to think so. He might act very foolishly indeed if he thought I was cooling my heels in the lock-up.'

Calshott smiled faintly again.

'You have a very ingenious mind, Major Dawlish,' he said with feeling. 'I must confess that I am relieved to find that you do not seriously believe the nonsense you talked about me. Bligh, check up with Corbett and Waring, will you?'

Bligh left quickly and Calshott sat down, still toying with the pencil as he regarded Trivett.

'I was startled to hear that the Yard had been consulted, even informally, Superintendent. It appears that Bligh, perhaps with some justification, was nervous of pursuing inquiries when they so obviously centred around my company. He need not have been, I would gladly have given him every facility for investigation. However, be that as it may—Major Dawlish has not allowed the situation to remain static.'

'Nice of you,' murmured Dawlish.

'And he has produced a remarkable chain of circumstantial evidence pointing towards my company,' Calshott said. 'Have you anything to add to that, Superintendent?'

'At the moment, no,' said Trivett.

'I see. And, assuming that your suspicions of me *are* imaginary,' Calshott said drily to Dawlish, 'what other ideas have you to discuss, Major Dawlish?'

Dawlish shrugged. 'Someone at the company offices knows why Mildred Gay and her boy-friend died,' he said. 'Tentative inquiries there might be useful, but I still think we'll get results through Dickerson quicker than anyone else—if we handle him properly. Merely a suggestion, but if he were let off with a caution and the belief that I myself am under suspicion, I think it might bring results. There is no apparent evidence against him, of course—he's always been very careful to make sure of that. However, it must exist, so we will be able to find it.'

He stopped short as the door burst open and Bligh rushed into the room.

'Sorry, sir! Dickerson'—the Inspector gulped for breath—'Dickerson has broken away—he—he assaulted the sergeant and left ten minutes ago.'

Calshott stared, wide-eyed. Trivett thrust his hands deep in his pockets, while Dawlish looked at them all with the beginning of a grin.

'It worked, you see,' he said. 'Panic aroused in Dickerson's guilty breast, assault on a police-sergeant is a charge good enough to bring him in under compulsion. Not bad,' he added, gently. 'Not at all bad—and as Dickerson has decided to do it this way, there won't be any need to lock me up.'

Calshott pressed the pencil against a blotting pad so heavily that the point snapped. He flung the pencil away from him and said, sharply:

'You must find him, Bligh! And immediate inquiries must be made at my offices. Superintendent, this is very informal, I know, but I would appreciate your assistance while you're here—I hope your own business isn't more pressing?'

'Not at all, sir,' said Trivett. 'Only too pleased.'

There was not a great deal that Trivett could do immediately, for the inquiries at the S.W.W.D.C. were better carried out, in the original stages, by Bligh and his men. There remained the interrogation of the man who had shot at Dawlish at the *George*, but he proved extremely uncommunicative and Dawlish wished again that he could have discussed the matter with the gunman out of the hearing of the police. That being impossible, he had to accept a sullen refusal to talk, and left the police station with Trivett some three quarters of an hour after that worthy's arrival, Calshott having appeared to have forgotten that there were charges to be investigated against him.

The early evening was warm, and when Dawlish and Trivett walked along to the *George* the streets of Terne were almost deserted; certainly no one showed any interest in them. Corbett, they knew, remained at the *George*. He had not been seriously hurt, but apparently his encounter with the gunman had caused a temporary relapse—he was nothing like so fit a man as he looked. He and Waring had corroborated Dawlish's story, as well as Simpson, who had been telephoned from the station.

So there was reason enough for Dawlish's smile as he walked by Trivett's side. Nor did Trivett's caustic remarks send the smile away.

'One day,' he said, 'you'll overstep the mark, Pat, and find yourself in a hole where I can't help you. Why the blazes did you go so bald-headed for Calshott? And why did you have to let Bligh down?'

'Taking the latter first, it was your fault and Bligh's,' Dawlish told him, 'you kept too much to yourself. You could have told me that Bligh had contacted you, and that because you were unable to do much officially you picked on me. That's the truth, isn't it?'

'Yes,' said Trivett, 'but you needn't have said so in front of Calshott.'

'I had no choice,' Dawlish said, 'at the time I didn't know that Fel had telephoned for you and I was trying to work myself out of a spot. For it *was* one, and a pretty nasty one.'

'You got yourself into it,' Trivett said, unkindly.

'Oh, no,' said Dawlish. 'It was a manoeuvre of Dickerson's. He was more than anxious to have me out of the way. I think he would have been satisfied if he'd succeeded even for a few hours, which suggests that things might happen in those hours.'

Trivett frowned. 'Well, what do you suggest we do?'

'Several things,' said Dawlish. 'Whatever else, Bill, I have managed to make 'em move. So amateurs do get there sometimes! Er—there's one little thing which I didn't like to say in front of Calshott.'

'You surprise me!' Trivett said drily.

'I mean, I didn't like to repeat it in front of Calshott,' said the large man, gently. 'I think he's probably in it, Bill, and I had him scared. I couldn't have over-ridden his authority, but he was doing some quick thinking. Now he's falling back on his prepared defences. Dickerson ran because he was afraid I would pursue the Calshott angle, and Calshott was greatly relieved when Bligh burst in with the gladsome tidings. My man's Calshott, William!'

CHAPTER TWENTY

NO OBJECTIONS FROM TRIVETT

'I suppose you're serious,' Trivett said at last.

'Of course I'm serious. Bligh must have had fair grounds for his suspicions, so must you, to have worked this trick on me.'

'Have you any evidence greater than a guess?' asked Trivett.

'No,' said Dawlish, frankly.

'Nor has Bligh and nor have I,' said Trivett. 'It's no small thing to suspect a Chief Constable of this kind of thing, you know, and it needs very strong proof.'

'No proof needed for suspicions,' murmured Dawlish.

'You know what I mean,' said Trivett, shortly.

'I wish I did,' said Dawlish. 'Even now, after I've nearly faced a charge of murder for you, you haven't told me *all* you know. What do you know, Bill?'

Trivett looked at him thoughtfully, but said nothing until they were in the *George*. Some time was lost while Felicity greeted Trivett and introduced Sheila. Then Dawlish explained, briefly, just what part Sheila had played. Felicity realised that it was dinner-time and suggested that they made their way to the dining-room. She and Sheila went ahead of the men while Dawlish regarded the Yard man hopefully.

'Now that Felicity has displayed her usual remarkable tact, what about it, Bill?'

'What do you want to know?'

'Bluntly, I want to know why you and Bligh suspect Calshott. What's it all about? I've unearthed a few oddments and connected 'em with the milk, but it's not enough. I know you well enough to know that you would not take this interest and get a Home Office letter for a trifling affair. Not that it is trifling, but most of the murders were still to come when you roused me into showing an interest. I—oh, damn!' he exclaimed, suddenly straightening up. 'I've forgotten Dippy Fowler!'

'Is he down here?' Trivett asked, in some surprise.

'He has been. Felicity was going to try to get in touch with him—he wanted a word with me,' Dawlish added. 'But first things first—what's the great suspicion?'

Trivett said: 'You've no idea?'

'None. Don't tell me that it's one of those things so large that you can't see 'em for looking.'

'I don't think it's that,' said Trivett, slowly. 'As you'd got as far as Calshott, I thought you might have gone further. Early in the war, Calshott was suspected of fascist tendencies and was questioned. He had been sympathetic towards the Nazi and Fascist regimes but appeared to have suffered a change of heart and so nothing was done. He's done nothing at all to suggest that it wasn't the right decision—in fact he's been a very useful man on the agricultural boards down here and his Company is among the best in the country. He subsidises many of the local farmers, makes sure they have the best cattle—' Trivett paused, smiling a little. 'Not very helpful?'

'If this were two years ago,' said Dawlish, 'or even one, I'd suggest that you had an idea he was hoping to receive a large German landing around here. It would explain the lime pits, they could be used for hiding key-men. Or, alternatively, that he was sheltering a party of Huns who were waiting for reinforcements. After all, they would need milk in their tea.'

Trivett looked at him curiously.

'Yes? Not often you're so slow, Pat.'

'Damn it, where's the lead?' asked Dawlish.

'We do suspect that Calshott, or someone else, is sheltering a party of Nazis and Fascists,' Trivett said. 'We were talking about it when I had lunch with you at the club.'

'Stop!' cried Dawlish, and eyed the policeman with growing astonishment. 'Bill, Bill, you *told* me what it was about!'

'I went as near as I could,' said Trivett, 'or rather, as near as I dared—I suggested that you would probably be the right man to help us, but I couldn't get permission to tell you the whole story.' He laughed, but without amusement. 'No, I was not interested in the weather over the Straits of Dover, the respective merits of British Overseas and Pan-American Airways, or the Chancellor of the Exchequer, but I *was* interested in the rumour that a couple of dozen Nazis, aiming for Eire, had been lost in the English Channel. The reports about the 'plane being shot down were circumstantial enough, but—there were doubts. I don't think it was shot down into the sea. I think the party landed somewhere near here—we've searched the country and the only places where parts of a machine otherwise unaccounted for have been discovered have been within reasonable distance of Terne.'

Dawlish thought of the pieces of metal on Bligh's desk. 'Bligh told me, too,' he said. When Trivett did not comment, he added: 'A couple of dozen of Hitler's thugs trying to get out while the going is good and heading for Eire in the hope that they'll be able to ship to the South American continent—is that it? All of them somewhere in this district and being fed—and supplied with milk!' He drew a deep breath. 'You suspect Calshott because you knew of his earlier pro-German sympathies?'

'Yes—so did Bligh.'

'Why the blazes was such a man allowed to remain as Chief Constable?'

'There wasn't any evidence on which to remove him,' said Trivett. 'The same could be said of others in authority, you know, even pro-Nazi politicians. They were the appeasers, perhaps, but not traitors. Calshott's been watched carefully, of course, and until the past few weeks there's been nothing at all to suggest that he wasn't wholly sincere. Then parts of a German transport machine were found in the river and in some of the fields not far from here. Soon afterwards the Dickerson housekeepers gave me an excuse for seeing Bligh. We suspected Dickerson and Brett but could find nothing to justify it. I think,' he added, 'that you were about right when you said that Dickerson acted as he did to attract attention and distract it from the major issue.'

'Well, well,' said Dawlish, blankly.

'We still haven't the slightest evidence that the party is near here,' went on Trivett. 'We have only the evidence that milk has been missing as well as other commodities sold by the S.W.W.D.C. It is a farming district, so it wouldn't be difficult to get enough food for them. The question is—are they near here? and if so, where? I think at least one of the housekeepers discovered that Dickerson, Brett and—possibly—Calshott, were helping Nazi fugitives to get out of the country.'

He paused, then went on:

'If I'm right, these men are near here and might get away. We want 'em and we intend to get 'em.' He went on slowly: 'There's only a narrow strip of Devon between Dayshire and the coast and it wouldn't be difficult on dark nights for them to get away.'

'And not a word of this has been breathed to anyone?'

'It has not! Imagine what harm it would do if it were thought that England was being used as a stepping stone for these swine to escape.'

Dawlish nodded thoughtfully. 'I wonder if that was what Dippy Fowler wanted to tell me about—he's no fool, little though I like him. All the same, Bill—surely your hand was strong enough to force Calshott to answer questions?'

'No proof,' said Trivett briefly. 'We have to envisage the possibility that we're wrong, after all. Everything was done very quietly, pieces were fitted together, but we couldn't break anything open. Whitehall is so anxious that there shouldn't be a leakage that I wasn't even allowed to tell you about it, or inform your Department. However, you *would* have been told but for one thing.'

'And what was that?'

'Getting married,' said Trivett, smiling a little. 'If you'd been on your own I could have got permission to tell you at the last minute, but they didn't trust you not to tell Felicity, and they didn't believe she would be proof against passing it on. After all, even if you had known, what else could you have done? This had to be broken open from the Dickerson end, not Calshott's. You've worried Calshott all right,' he added with a reflective smile, 'and he might be forced into taking some kind of precipitate action, but the most likely angle still seems to be Dickerson.'

'Ah,' said Dawlish. 'Yes. Couldn't a house-to-house search be made?'

'Every house large enough to hold them has already been visited,' Trivett said. 'If they're here, it's my belief that they're living somewhere underground.'

'Oh, well,' said Dawlish. 'I—'

He stopped abruptly.

'Now what?' demanded Trivett.

'Tin mines,' said Dawlish.

'They're being worked,' said Trivett sourly.

'*Some* are, perhaps, not all,' said Dawlish. 'Bill, find me a disused tin mine, will you?'

Somewhat deflated, Dawlish listened as the Yard man told him again that all the obvious possibilities had been explored. There were known to be five disused tin mines in that part of the country and on the pretext that they might be re-opened under Government order they had all been inspected; nothing suspicious had been found.

Dawlish thereupon declared that he had never been able to think on an empty stomach and that it was time they went downstairs.

They found Corbett talking animatedly to Sheila.

Dawlish eyed him thoughtfully; a nephew of Calshott, on the spot at Grange Farm, he might be responsible for the milk shortages, for the lime—which had doubtless been obtained from one of the nearby farms—and for other things.

Everything pointed to the fact that the seat of the trouble was near Wood Grange. But there had been no hidden party of fugitive Nazis in Dickerson's house, and Bligh had telephoned Trivett to say that Brett's house had also been thoroughly searched again, to no avail.

Calshott, it seemed, was doing everything he could to assist the investigations at the Company's office and factory. The manager, Waring, was there and the police were going through books, accounts, and records in the hope of finding out what had been discovered by the girl and the lorry driver;

but by twelve o'clock that night, nothing suspicious had been found.

Nor was there any trace of Dickerson.

The Home Guard, military and police units searching the countryside around Terne, had been supplemented by two mining-experts, brought from the nearest working mines, to investigate the possibility that there was a hidden shaft somewhere in the hillside. Five lime-pits had been found in all.

All of these things Dawlish told Felicity, a little after midnight, fresh from another interview with Trivett and Bligh—the latter, he said, seemed relieved that the secret was out and inclined, now, to discredit the possibility that Calshott was involved.

Corbett had gone to his cottage, where for extra security, Bligh had placed two policemen. Simpson's farm was also watched—a protective measure upon which Bligh had insisted.

'So,' said Felicity, sitting up in bed and watching Dawlish as he brushed his hair, 'you're not much further forward, Pat?'

'Well, we've made *some* progress,' Dawlish said. 'The secrecy angle was annoying, but I suppose it was necessary. Er— one thing, Fel. You're sure you couldn't find a trace of Dippy Fowler?'

'There wasn't a sign of him,' Felicity assured him.

It appeared that since Fowler had left Dawlish in the crowded yard of the *George*, he had vanished. Regretting deeply that he had not been able to talk to the man, Dawlish sighed and went to bed.

A maid called them, with tea, at eight o'clock. They were drinking it when there was a tap at the door and Sheila appeared. She was fully dressed and looked exceedingly happy.

'You've been out early,' Dawlish said.

'I woke up about six and couldn't get to sleep again,' said Sheila, 'so I went for a stroll.'

'And what time does Bruce Corbett bring the milk in to Terne?' demanded Dawlish, drily.

Sheila laughed. 'About seven o'clock!'

'And I trust he is well,' said Dawlish.

'I wish he were fitter than he is,' said Sheila, with unexpected gravity, 'but—' she broke off.

'He's fit enough,' Dawlish said robustly. 'Now do take your mind off him for ten seconds and set it to work on my problem. After all, you were housekeeper to Dickerson for the better part of twelve hours, you ought to know *some*thing.'

'But I've told you everything,' Sheila assured him lightly. 'I—oh!'

'Hallo, here it comes,' said Dawlish. 'What have you forgotten to tell me?'

'I don't know why I've forgotten,' Sheila admitted, 'and it may not mean much. He said that if a man named Cartwright were to come to the house, he would always be at home. That's all'

Dawlish said, thoughtfully. 'Cartwright. He didn't describe him?'

'No—he just gave the name.'

Dawlish said pessimistically: 'Probably said to mislead, and there's no such man. Still, Bligh had better know. There *might* be a Cartwright in this business somewhere. Cartwright, Cartwright,' he repeated. 'Oh, forget it!' he added, with a touch of exasperation. 'It's time I got up!'

When Dawlish had bathed and dressed, he telephoned Bligh. There were no results from the search at the Milk Company offices nor at the factory which had been visited during the night.

Calshott, Bligh said, had been up most of the night and had been remarkably helpful; so had Trivett, who had obtained a room at another hotel but not gone there until after five o'clock.

Bligh gave the impression that he and Trivett felt very glum, particularly because of Dickerson's escape.

'No need to be too depressed about it,' Dawlish said, 'it merely means that he hasn't gone far. Nothing else?'

'Nothing at all,' Bligh assured him.

'You haven't seen anything of that London reporter I was talking about last night?'

'No,' said Bligh. 'I took the trouble to telephone his office. Apparently he was sent down here, when it was learned that you had arrived, to see if he could get another story on the Dickerson business. He hasn't reported since he left London.'

'Oh. Well, I'd better—but wait a moment! Does the name "Cartwright" mean anything to you?'

Bligh pondered for a moment and then said that it did not.

'I was afraid of that,' said Dawlish. 'Nothing from Corbett's cottage or Simpson's farm?'

'Were you expecting anything?'

'No, but nothing would surprise me,' said Dawlish.

He said good-bye and rang off, in no better frame of mind than when he had woken up. He took himself to task, for he was no companion for Felicity in such a mood.

He joined her in the entrance hall, tucked her arm under his and led her into the High Street. She took a quick glance at his set profile.

'Another idea, Pat?'

'One I don't like,' Dawlish said, shortly.

'Can I hear about it?'

'Ye-es. Fel, these housekeepers started disappearing over three months ago.'

'Hm-hm,' said Felicity.

'The 'plane load of fugitives didn't arrive until a few days ago.'

'Ye-es.'

'The milk shortage has been going on for some weeks—just how long, I gather, Waring doesn't know. It was discovered a fortnight ago and has been checked several times since.'

'Well?' said Felicity

'It doesn't tie-up with a recent 'plane load. If the fugitive angle is the right one, there have been other parties. A regular traffic, in fact.'

'Ye-es,' conceded Felicity.

'That would fit in with Trivett's deep interest and the hush-hush attitude. A single load of men would be a sensation, a general and regular trickle of them would be a scandal of the first degree. Dickerson's reputation was forced down the throats of the natives, he did nothing at all to escape it. When Dippy Fowler's article appeared, he seemed to derive some amusement and continued to ask for more. The milk shortages, all the other things, including the shooting and the attempt to kill Sheila— all very obvious. All making sure that we concentrate on Terne, of course. Even the evidence pointing towards Calshott and the Dairy Company has been obvious and—because Mildred Gay was dressed in one of the housekeeper's clothes—it was done deliberately to make us connect it with Dickerson and Terne.'

'Ye-es,' said Felicity.

'Peculiar,' said Dawlish. 'Everything points to Terne. Dickerson even runs away from Terne when he wants to make it look as if the game is up. Clever people, these. Aeroplane parts of German manufacture, evidence that it was a transport 'plane and yet no sign of the scene of the crash. Just the obvious evidence to get us here and to make us look here. It *could* be one enormous bluff, my sweet.'

Felicity said slowly:

'Do you mean that the fugitives have never been near Terne? That it's all been done to make us think they have?'

'That is precisely what I mean,' said Dawlish, sombrely. He paused, looked across the road, and saw a chemist's shop. 'I think,' he added, 'that I'm going to need aspirins for the worst headache of my misspent life!'

CHAPTER TWENTY-ONE

DAWLISH GETS ANOTHER IDEA

Dawlish duly bought the aspirins and he and Felicity went back to the *George* to breakfast. Felicity returned to the subject quietly.

'Pat, if it's not Terne, where is it? I mean, have you any idea?'

'One,' said Dawlish, slowly, 'which might help.'

'What's that?'

'Dippy Fowler,' Dawlish said soberly. 'He knew something, and tried to tell me so. Someone in the crowd heard him and he was taken away. Neat and in keeping with the speed and precision with which these people work. Everything arranged so that the police *had* to concentrate on Terne—even Brett's connection with the Milk Company worked in beautifully.' He brooded for a moment and then added: 'So we come back to the inevitable questions—where's Fowler? What does he know?'

Felicity nodded, without speaking.

'There's another thing,' said Dawlish. 'Maude and the other maids of the house disappeared pretty quickly don't you think?—I suspect that Dickerson paid 'em off, but they ought to be found and questioned, no doubt about that.'

'Now steady, Pat,' said Felicity. 'You asked Bligh to do that last night—even if you hadn't, he would have thought of it for himself.'

'Hum, yes,' said Dawlish. He made a face and then stood up, his eyes restless and worried. 'I might even be wrong about Calshott. And Waring.'

'Pat, are you doing any good going on like this?' demanded Felicity.

'I don't know,' said Dawlish, 'but if I talk enough I might get an idea.' He smiled unhappily. 'I'd better go to the station and bore them instead of you.'

Outside the police station he met Trivett, and told him how his mind had worked. Trivett said enough to make it clear that he, too, had vague suspicions of some such enormous hoax, conceived to side-track all investigation.

'But if you're right, why did they worry to set us thinking about this place at all?' asked Trivett, helplessly.

Dawlish looked morosely along the street, frowning because he heard a sound which had unpleasant associations; it was the rumbling of a tank going along the High Street. It passed and several others followed, together with a motor-cycle and two armoured cars and a jeep. The large white star of the U.S.A.A.F. were painted on the sides of the vehicles.

Dawlish frowned and said, slowly:

'Bill, that's odd.'

'What's odd?' asked Trivett.

'The one thing we've taken for granted, the one story we haven't doubted. The way that tank appeared and went over the edge of the hillside. Remarkable.'

'You think so?'

'We-ell, I wonder if the local C.O. has been in touch with Bligh about that tank? Come on! Let's find out!'

Trivett was not impressed by the sudden burst of energy, and Dawlish was already in Bligh's office talking to the startled Terne man, when he reached the doorway. Bligh was saying:

'I've heard nothing more than that—the lieutenant in charge of the unit told me it would be reported to his Commanding Officer.'

'No effort has been made to remove the tank?'

'None,' said Bligh. 'I haven't had much time to think about it, of course, and—'

'What are you getting heated about, Pat?' asked Trivett.

'And you're a policeman!' exclaimed Dawlish. 'Bill, when a tank falls over a cliff like that, within an hour the telephones should be humming, every Tom, Dick, and Harry in the Local Command should be wanting to know something about it. There *should* have been a delegation here within an hour of it being reported, yet—*nothing's* happened, nothing at all!'

'Well, just because they've been slack—' Trivett began.

'*Slack?*' repeated Dawlish. 'The accident hasn't been reported to Local Command Headquarters. 'Phone 'em and see—they'd be at Salisbury, wouldn't they? Salisbury, Salisbury,' he repeated, 'Ted Beresford is there!' Without a by-your-leave he picked up the telephone, and gave a Salisbury number. After a short wait, he asked for Captain Beresford. There was another delay, while Dawlish said to Trivett:

'That was a phoney unit, Bill, I should never have believed in a soldier who left his post because someone cried "help"—I should have followed it up. The whole unit's phoney, d'you understand? Don't spread the story about but get the local Home Guard people busy, find out what part of the hillside the so-called army unit covered and what part was left to the Home Guard . . . Hallo, is that you Ted?'

'Someone sounds excited,' said Ted Beresford, whose absence

Dawlish had regretted early in the affair. 'Pat, I'm hurt to the quick! No wedding cake!'

'Has anyone reported a tank which crashed over a hill at Terne?' asked Dawlish, urgently.

'Tank at Terne?' asked Beresford bewilderedly. 'No word's reached me—is it urgent?'

'Nothing was ever more so,' Dawlish said.

'All right, hold on and I'll have a word with our tank man,' said Beresford, and began to talk into another telephone. Dawlish waited in a frenzy of impatience before Beresford came on the line again; it had been a very long wait and Bligh had left the office.

'There haven't been any British tank units in Terne for several months,' said Beresford, 'only U.S.A.'

'Is that absolutely certain?'

'Oh, yes, there's no doubt,' said Beresford. 'There are a few units, mostly Pioneer Corps and some infantry at Terne Camp, but it's practically closed up. Tanks haven't been there for several months. There were some obsolete tanks left there—the engines dismantled and only the hulks remaining. But Pat, you'll have to explain what—'

'Now listen to me carefully,' said Dawlish.

He talked rapidly for two minutes then, refusing to be delayed any longer, rang off. He looked significantly at Trivett.

'So I haven't lost my head, Bill. They impersonate a British Army unit in England—and who is to question them? Some forged papers, authority enough to satisfy any local bigwigs who ask questions and the C.O.s of any other unit nearby—Terne Camp is practically deserted, no one of any consequence there. Uniforms wouldn't be difficult to arrange, the sight of a unit of men wandering about by day or night, or sleeping under canvas—who would be surprised? Who would ask questions?'

Trivett said soberly:

'Pat, if they've tanks they might have other armaments and ammunition.'

'It wouldn't surprise me,' admitted Dawlish, 'but now I've stirred the Salisbury Command into taking notice I don't think we need worry much about that, all we have to worry about is a holding action once we've located their present headquarters. A movable one, of course. What does Bligh think of the Home Guard about here?'

'A lot,' said Trivett, 'but—' he broke off, obviously deeply concerned.

'Cheer up,' said Dawlish, soothingly. 'If it's any comfort, Bill— and I mean this!—I think I know where the headquarters are.'

CHAPTER TWENTY-TWO

THE HILL AGAIN

Colonel North, the Commanding Officer of the 3rd Battalion of the Dayshire Home Guard was an ex-regular army officer who, in Bligh's opinion, was a very sound man indeed. Dawlish liked the look of him. He was tall, square-shouldered and ruddy of complexion; he knew nothing of what had been discovered and explained precisely how the Home Guard and the regular Army unit had divided up the search of the hillside after the crashing of the tank. He had taken that part nearer Wood Grange and the others the part at the back of the house, nearer to Dr. Brett's. As he pointed out, police officers had been in both sections, but the actual searching and inspection of the pits had been undertaken by the military.

'I'm quite sure nothing was missed by my fellows,' said North, 'but I wouldn't like to guarantee the others did a thorough job. In fact, I thought of saying so when I saw you today, Bligh.'

'Why was that?' asked Dawlish, quickly.

North shrugged.

'They were a raggle-taggle lot. My own fellows, twice their age, would have made twice the men. Mind you, I know that the best troops have gone overseas, but that unit—I imagine that they were all dullards who wouldn't or couldn't learn the rudiments of the business.'

Dawlish said quietly: 'You saw their officer's authority, I suppose?'

North stared at him.

'Of course. They had a lieutenant—not much better than the rest of them, from what I could see.'

'You didn't recognise any of them?'

'I was told they had only moved in a day or two before,' said North, 'and that wasn't surprising, units are always chopping and changing. I've often crossed the moor and seen units under canvas without having been told that they were there. I'm supposed to be advised when a new unit is coming, but—' North shrugged. 'Well, things don't always work out according to plan.'

'They certainly don't,' said Dawlish. Briefly he told North what he believed to be the truth. The Colonel was incredulous at first, but his own voluntary statement had given weight to Dawlish's suggestions; when he heard of the information from Salisbury, he threw up his hands.

'I don't think there can be any doubt, then. What do you want me to do?'

'No histrionics, no gnashing of teeth', thought Dawlish, 'he's going to be all right.' Aloud, he asked: 'What area does the site of the camp cover?'

'If you mean where are units stationed now,' said North, 'there's one about a mile and a half from Wood Grange—the unit which worked with us yesterday. I know it's still there because I was up on the moor this morning.'

'How many strong?' asked Dawlish.

'Forty or fifty men, at a guess.'

'Can you cut 'em off from the rest of the district?'

North whistled. 'It'll take some doing, but with help from the police I think it can be managed.'

'We'll do our share,' said Bligh, quickly.

'You won't want to lose any time,' North said. 'I'd better get things going. I suppose you don't want it too widely known?'

'I don't want it known at all,' Dawlish said.

'I've got to get my men together and they come from all over the town,' North pointed out. 'It won't take long for word to get round that the Home Guard has been called out.'

Dawlish shrugged. 'Do the best you can, will you? But before you go, tell me just where you saw the unit this morning?'

North gave him explicit directions and Dawlish smiled his thanks before the Colonel left, leaving Dawlish, Trivett, and Bligh in the latter's office.

'I *ought* to tell the Chief Constable,' Bligh said, eyeing Dawlish doubtfully.

'Leave it for half an hour, will you?' Dawlish said quietly. 'I hope it wasn't necessary to tell North to block the roads at the foot of the hills,' he added. 'You'll work direct with him, Bligh?'

'Oh, yes,' said the Terne inspector.

'Good!' Dawlish smiled, and rose to go. 'Coming, Bill?'

'What are you going to do, Pat?' asked Trivett as they left the station.

'Go up and have a look around,' said Dawlish, promptly. 'But you're not coming with me, Bill. There's no need for you to and I want someone to make sure that Fel and Sheila don't run around loose—I can't keep an eye on them if I'm hunting Huns on the moor.'

Trivett hesitated, then said firmly: 'I think we'll both go. I've brought a sergeant with me, he'll look after Felicity and Sheila.'

Dawlish shrugged. 'I suppose I can't stop you if you're set on it.'

'Aren't you seeing Felicity before you start?'

'Yes,' said Dawlish, 'but you're not, you might give the game away! I'll pick you up at the foot of the hill.'

On his own, Dawlish strode along the High Street with a ferocious scowl on his face. He was not surprised to find Felicity and Sheila in the foyer of the *George*, nor was he surprised by the alarm on Felicity's face and the apprehension on Sheila's. He said nothing, but motioned them to the stairs.

'Where's Corbett?' He asked, as soon as they were in the bedroom.

'He's gone to report for work,' said Sheila. 'To Simpson, I mean. Pat, what's the matter?'

Dawlish said harshly:

'They've got away. They were in the hills but moved out during the night. We've got things going and there's a widespread search for 'em, but I'm afraid we've missed 'em.'

Felicity said nothing at all.

'I'm going to Brett's house with Trivett,' Dawlish said, 'there's just a chance that we'll find something on the second search. I should be back before eleven. Or twelve, at the latest,' he added, quickly. 'I've an appointment in town with Sir Mortimer Calshott.'

'So it *is* Calshott,' Felicity said, slowly.

'It wouldn't surprise me,' Dawlish said, smiling grimly, 'but it'd be safer, I think, if you stayed here. I don't think there'll be any more trouble, as it looks as if for once we've arrived too late, but they might be spiteful and work up a revengeful act. If I'm later than twelve I'll 'phone you.' He kissed Felicity, patted Sheila's arm, and went out.

Once in the passage he heaved a sigh of relief.

Doubtless Felicity would, if she knew, be put out by his deception, but he thought he had put up a convincing case, and relieved her of immediate anxiety. Of all things, he wanted to make sure that she did not follow him to the moors. He took out the M.G., and drove off rapidly. At the foot of the hill he picked up Trivett.

Meanwhile strange things were happening in Terne.

The Home Guard, armed with rifles and sub-machine guns were moving through the streets. Dawlish and Trivett found that a barrier had been put across the road at a corner on the hill. It was well-guarded and they would have had difficulty in getting past had not North been at hand. Cheered by this evidence of thoroughness on the part of the H.G. Commander, Dawlish sped on his way past the turning towards Wood Grange, where other Home Guards, reinforced with Bligh's policemen, were on duty. No one tried to stop them and Dawlish saw that North had planned to lure the unit—*if* it moved out—down the hill, so that his men could close in behind.

'Where are you thinking of going—or shouldn't I ask?' demanded Trivett, tartly.

'Where but the moor?' asked Dawlish, 'and if we happen to pass Corbett's cottage first, what of it?' He continued to drive at speed, until Corbett's cottage came in sight, when he pulled up with a flourish.

No one appeared.

'Why are you so interested in Corbett?' demanded Trivett.

'Sheer obstinacy,' said Dawlish, with a grin. 'Do you mind if we stay to look around?' The front door was ajar. He raised his voice and shouted for Corbett, but there was no answer. He hurried through to the kitchen; it was empty. They went up the stairs, the big man ahead of Trivett.

He found Corbett's bedroom neat and tidy, but unoccupied. Then he turned to the other door, immediately opposite; it was locked. The door was lightly enough built, and it did not take him long to break it down.

Dawlish stepped over the threshold—and stopped, staring. On the bed where he had once laid Dickerson, *Dippy Fowler* was lying, bound hand and foot.

CHAPTER TWENTY-THREE

EVIDENCE AGAINST CORBETT

When Dawlish had untied the cords, Fowler sat on the side of the bed, working his ankles and wrists and swearing audibly.

'How long have you been here?' Dawlish asked.

'All the perishing night,' growled Fowler, 'and it seems like a week! I was hustled into a car just after I'd tried to make you see some sense, Dawlish.'

'Ah,' said Dawlish. 'You succeeded, but I was late in looking for you.'

'Too late,' said Fowler, shooting Trivett an unfriendly glance. 'I suppose I ought to have expected that!'

'Such gratitude,' murmured Dawlish. 'Who brought you here?'

'A couple of roughnecks,' Fowler said. 'What does it matter! You've let 'em all go—Corbett and the lot of them.'

'Corbett?' said Dawlish, softly.

'I thought you'd twigged *that* at least,' snapped Fowler. 'Corbett's in this up to the neck. This is where he's provisioned the Huns.'

'So you know about them,' said Dawlish.

'So would anyone who wasn't a fool,' said Fowler. 'I came

down here last week to find out what I could about Dickerson and then I heard about the transport 'plane—I'm not a complete idiot.' He scowled. 'I started to look for Huns and discovered Corbett was lifting milk and provisions from one of the lorries which passed here every day. He worked in with the driver.'

Dawlish said: 'Are you sure they've gone?'

'They won't have lost any time,' said Fowler.

'Do you know where they were hidden?'

'I haven't a notion,' Fowler said. 'Have you?'

'A fair idea, yes,' said Dawlish, 'and I don't think they've all gone yet. Can you manage a little spin before you have something to eat?'

'If there's a drink in this place that'll do me.'

Dawlish led the way downstairs to the kitchen. Rummaging about in the cupboards Fowler found a half bottle of whisky. He poured himself out a liberal dose, drank it neat and then wiped his mouth with the back of his hand.

'I'm ready,' he said, 'where are you going?'

'To Simpson's farm.' said Dawlish.

The farmhouse looked serene and restful in the morning sun.

Some two miles away, moving slowly towards them, they could see a little convoy of army vehicles. Near Simpson's farm was a little armoured car, with two officers standing by it. A sergeant was coming out of the farmhouse and walking smartly towards the armoured car. In the doorway stood Simpson, he looked surprised as the M.G. came to a standstill and Dawlish climbed out, hurrying ahead of Fowler and Trivett.

Simpson greeted him with a puzzled smile.

'Good morning, Major Dawlish.'

'Good morning,' said Dawlish, gruffly. 'Have you seen Corbett?'

'Why, no,' said Simpson, as if surprised. 'I understood that he was staying in Terne.'

'You're sure you haven't seen Corbett this morning?'

'I said so,' said Simpson, stiffly.

'Have you seen Calshott?'

'Who?' Simpson ejaculated, wide-eyed.

'Calshott,' said Dawlish harshly. 'Sir Mortimer Calshott, Corbett's uncle.'

'Of course I haven't.'

'Look here, Dawlish—' began Fowler.

Dawlish snapped: 'I told you to be quiet!' He saw Trivett's troubled expression and the astonishment in the reporter's eyes. He went on, savagely: 'Fowler, you tried hard but not hard enough. You told us that you had been tied up on that bed for over twelve hours, but within five minutes you were walking about easily. The cords weren't tight, if you'd tried—and you would have tried had your story been genuine—you would have got free in an hour or less. You said you were starving—but half a tumbler of neat whisky didn't have any effect on you at all. It would have made you dizzy, hard toper though you are, if you hadn't eaten for twelve hours. Corbett knew nothing about you being there, it's part of a simple plan to make Corbett look guilty.'

Fowler gaped. 'You—you must be—'

'Don't say crazy,' said Dawlish, 'it's too hackneyed. Simpson— *where's Corbett?*'

The farmer said: 'I haven't any idea what you're talking about, Dawlish. Do you think this man—'

Dawlish said: 'Listen to me, Simpson. There are only a few houses about here which could serve as headquarters. I pointed that out to you when I called yesterday. Dickerson's has gone, Brett's is closely watched, Corbett's cottage is out—and that leaves *Grange Farm*. It is the only place of any size about here which has not been under police surveillance for weeks past. It's the only place where men could take shelter. Are you following me?'

'You are quite wrong,' Simpson said, slowly.

'Of course, it *might* have been used without your knowledge.' Trivett spoke suddenly, sharply.

'Pat, look behind you!'

Dawlish, turning swiftly, saw the two officers and the sergeant from the armoured car coming towards them—and the sergeant held a tommy-gun. It was obvious that the men were prepared to do murder then and there.

Fowler said in a strangled voice:

'You've asked for it, Dawlish. I—'

Dawlish's arm shot out. He grabbed Fowler by the wrist and dragged him into the doorway of the farmhouse. Trivett followed swiftly, with a violent blow he flung Simpson into the hall, slamming the door behind him. As he did so the stutter of the tommy-gun began to beat, bullets pecking into the stone portico.

Trivett had taken an automatic from his pocket and Dawlish the gun which he had taken from Dickerson.

The shooting outside stopped.

Dawlish smiled. 'Sorry, Bill, but I couldn't think of any other way of making 'em panic. With luck, North's men will be here soon and that will send the trio outside scuttling.'

'They might break in first,' Trivett said, in an even voice.

Dawlish's smile widened. 'Oh, no, Bill, they won't break in here, the place has been too heavily fortified. Steel shutters, all in place. Haven't you noticed? This door is solid enough to keep out tommy-gun bullets at twenty yards. Our danger comes from inside, not from out.

'*Dawlish!*' a man's voice hailed. '*Dawlish!*'

From upstairs there was an oath, a thud then a footstep. Dawlish moved to the side of the stairs, Trivett to the other side, Dawlish reflecting with an unnatural calm that it had been Corbett's voice that cried out, but that others were with him.

'Slip through to the back and make sure the door's locked, Bill, will you?' asked Dawlish. 'I think Simpson will have had everything ready in case of attack, but we ought to make sure.'

Trivett walked cautiously along the passage to the back of the house, while Dawlish watched the stairs.

No further sound came from the upper floors.

Trivett returned and said quietly:

'The doors and windows are all bolted and shuttered, Pat, there's no one in the rooms back there.'

'Is there a cellar?'

'I saw no sign of one.'

'Good! The trouble will come from the first floor. I wonder who's up there? Dickerson, for one. Calshott? I wonder.'

A bullet smashed through the bannister-struts. It missed Dawlish by a couple of feet and went nowhere near Trivett, but it was enough to warn them that the man, or men, upstairs were getting anxious. The stuttering of the tommy-gun came from outside again, but nothing forced its way through.

'On the whole, Bill, we aren't doing so badly,' Dawlish said. 'Dickerson upstairs, and unable to get out—did I tell you that all the windows are shuttered from outside, one of the little mistakes that Simpson and company made? With North and his Home Guards holding up the unit, the trio outside will soon realise that its time they hurried off and left Dickerson and the others to their fate.'

There was a pause before Dickerson's voice came from the landing.

'They won't go without us, Dawlish, you needn't think that you've got any chance—'

Dawlish said, as if surprised: 'Well, well, if it isn't Dickerson! Who's with you, little man?' Dickerson made no reply and Dawlish added: 'Why don't you make a rush for it? Or why don't you use one of those little incendiaries you're so fond of. Or a hand-grenade—don't say you haven't any.'

Trivett said: 'Shut up, you ass!'

Dawlish said: 'Not really an ass, Bill, if they had 'em they'd use 'em. Peculiar position, isn't it? All goes well while neither side does anything, but if we were to try to go upstairs or they were to try to come down—*then* the fur would fly. My only regret is for Corbett.'

He uttered the name softly, so that only Trivett could hear, but it was almost as if Dickerson could read his mind, for he called down:

'Dawlish, I'll make a bargain with you. Let us go, and Corbett will be unhurt.'

'Corbett will be unhurt in any case,' said Dawlish, grimly, 'because if he isn't, I'll deal with you before the police take you in hand, even if Trivett *is* standing beside me.'

His expression had altered, however; he knew the danger to Corbett and was desperately anxious to help the man.

Voices sounded from outside; the two 'lieutenants' and the 'sergeant' appeared to be presenting an ultimatum. Dawlish ignored them—and, after perhaps two minutes, there was a sullen roar and a heavy thud against the door. It shook the house, brought pictures crashing from the walls and sent ornaments flying from mantelpieces and shelves. A bulge appeared in the door; and then the light went out.

Softly, Dawlish said:

'The big gun of the armoured car, Bill.'

Trivett said nothing.

'But North's men will hear it and send a detachment over,' Dawlish nodded, calmly enough.

Trivett said grimly: 'I hope you're right.'

It was unnerving to wait for the second shot, to know that they could not defend themselves, to know that if they allowed Dickerson and whoever was with him to go out, it would probably save their own lives.

A second shot crashed against the door. It needed only one, perhaps two, more, for the door to fall.

Again a crash came, and the whole house shook. A gap appeared, high up on the left side of the door.

Crash! The house shook again, and this time the door sagged and gave way.

There was a moment of utter silence.

Dawlish, anticipating that there would be a rush for the stairs, stood shoulder to shoulder with Trivett, both men crouching forward, their guns in their hands.

CHAPTER TWENTY-FOUR

TWO DAYS FOR A HONEYMOON

When it came, there was something to be admired in the rush and the courage which made it possible. Dickerson came first, firing from an automatic; beyond Dickerson came a short stocky man whose bullet head proclaimed his Germanic origin. He, too, fired, missing Dawlish by inches.

It was easy enough at such close range to bring both men down.

Footsteps sounded from above, and a guttural mutter to an unseen personage addressed as:

'Excellency.'

The next moment the man leapt, almost sailing between Dawlish and Trivett's fire, landed on the broken door and made his escape.

Wild and somewhat confused shots passed from either side. The door of the armoured car was open. A few of the wounded men reached it. Slowly it began to move, running unsteadily over the meadow-land beyond the low front wall.

Trivett joined Dawlish, but did not speak.

'They almost deserve to escape,' Dawlish said, 'but I don't think they'll get far.'

The armoured car tore towards Terne and the hill, obviously the driver knew that the way was blocked behind him. Dawlish saw the shooting from the Home Guards and the smaller armoured cars coming towards it.

The pirate car began to fire, the red of the flame and the roar of the explosion coming clearly back to Dawlish's ears. But the single shot was a signal to the other cars—North, it seemed had managed to contact regular army units, almost certainly sent by Salisbury. Five of them fired, almost on the instant. Dawlish did not know how many shots hit the pirate, but he saw pieces flying from it in all directions. It slewed round, stopped—and then burst into flames.

Dawlish rubbed his chin, slowly.

'So, we held 'em up long enough, Bill,' he said. 'Now I wonder which of these johnnies will talk?'

Simpson was the first to break down. Dickerson and Fowler tried to stop him, but to no avail. Upstairs, Corbett lay unconscious with an ugly wound in his temple, but he was alive, and Dawlish did not think the wound would prove fatal.

Simpson spoke simply and obviously with full knowledge. It appeared that he and Dickerson, with help from Brett, had started the organisation which had concentrated on helping escaping Nazis and Fascists to get out of England once they had landed there, thinking—and rightly—that it would be the last place anyone would look for them.

One or two transport 'planes laden with fugitive Huns had landed, some of them had been smuggled into Eire and on to South America. There was no record of who they were. Carefully Dickerson had built himself up a reputation which, it was believed, would distract the attention of the police from the major purpose of the organisation. It had been realised that one day suspicions would be aroused and carefully attention had been drawn to Calshott's company, skilfully directed towards Calshott himself because of his earlier fascist sympathies.

'Calshott's not in it, then?' Dawlish asked.

'No,' said Simpson, 'he knew nothing of it. Bligh was made to think he was, we believed that we could persuade the police to concentrate on the milk factory while we hid the more important men here. But too many came over, we couldn't hide them indefinitely. One 'plane fell to bits as it landed and we had to collect every part we could find, although some were found and taken to the police. We couldn't keep two or three dozen men here without arousing suspicion, but Dickerson thought of stealing clothes from the stores at the camp. It was easy enough by night. There were old tanks about, obsolete and without engines, but we managed to put them together and got them in working order. Then we made up the "unit", which moved from place to place, never staying in the same district long, although always within easy reach of here.'

'Go on,' said Dawlish, slowly.

'The important thing, when inquiries started, was to make sure the army unit was not suspected,' said Simpson. 'Dickerson, as I say, worked up his particular scheme to draw your fire, with Calshott as a second line of defence; it didn't matter what the police thought provided they didn't suspect the truth.'

'No,' said Dawlish, 'but Dickerson went too far with the housekeepers. It wasn't necessary for him to advertise for *four*.'

Simpson said: 'Haven't you realised what happened? *The first housekeeper came from Germany*. She spoke English and no one suspected her; she was smuggled out of the country. Dickerson advertised for another housekeeper and then a second fugitive from Germany was given the job; she went away, too.'

Dawlish stared. 'My oath, that was clever!'

'Was it?' asked Simpson. 'I'm not so sure. Identities were manufactured for them, of course, and the Press started to make close inquiries, as well as the police. A third advertisement was put out and a genuine applicant, a Mrs. Bryant, was given the job—there wasn't work for her, really, but it was done to make the post seem genuine. She began to show a rather close interest in various curious happenings. One day she heard Dickerson and an unknown man talking fluent German. She was caught trying to telephone the police, and killed. Her body was put on a milk lorry. The driver discovered it and was bribed to keep silent. To carry on the pretence a fourth advertisement was inserted. That was after Fowler had been down here and, for a consideration, agreed to help us by concentrating the attention of the police on Dickerson and making it look as if he were a kind of modern Bluebeard.' Simpson shrugged. 'Whether it was wise or not it certainly succeeded for a while. Then you came, Dawlish, and had Dickerson guessing. We had a particularly high Nazi official here—von Richton,' Simpson added, wearily. 'Understudy to Rosenberg the Jew-baiter, wanted more badly than most of them. Dickerson had started his elaborate hide-and-seek and you forced him to keep it up.'

Simpson paused and drew his hand across his forehead.

'Corbett was always a danger, but I don't think he suspected that I was in it, especially as I pretended to hate Dickerson. My wife was a party to it, of course. Well—what else do you want to know?'

'What about the lorry driver?' Dawlish asked.

'I arranged with him—on Dickerson's request—to be outside the drive of Wood Grange, ready for you,' said Simpson. 'After that plot failed he panicked and was killed in an accident which we staged. Earlier, his girl had learned something of what had happened. We tried to bribe her but she wouldn't agree and she had to go. Dickerson tried to confuse the issue by dressing her in the clothes of the one genuine housekeeper he had employed up to then.'

Dawlish said: 'Too much finesse, my friend.'

'Far too much,' said Simpson, 'but we didn't know which way to turn. Your cousin was there long enough to be dangerous. One of the Nazis, in English uniform, came to see Dickerson— the fool spoke in German. We thought she heard him. Dickerson was scared by that time, and said she had to be killed. We arranged to do it by using some of the fugitives who were hiding about the hill; had they been found they could have given a good account of themselves, being in uniform. When that didn't work we tried the tank. We knew that if you really believed the Germans were here you would bring strong forces of military and keep the whole district under control. We were determined to move the unit, *en masse*, down to the coast. A small ship will be waiting tonight.' He stopped and smiled bitterly. 'The truth is, Dawlish, that you set the pace too high. We did everything we could to keep you off, even tried to frame you for Brett's murder. But it was no good.'

Dawlish said: 'Why did you do it, Simpson?'

Simpson shrugged. 'The pay was good,' he said. 'I thought I could get away with it. It was simple enough to give shelter to one or two, but when the Nazis began to panic and started coming in droves, it grew too big.'

'One other thing, Simpson—how did you manage to divert suspicion to Calshott?'

'We knew that he had been interrogated early in the war,' Simpson said, 'and Dickerson made a point of once or twice, visiting him at his home, knowing Bligh was aware of it. Calshott isn't a man to confide in his subordinates, so Bligh put two and two together and made five. The other evidence against Calshott was incidental, no more than that. We hoped to switch on to Corbett, the more likely man, at the last minute.'

'Well, well,' said Dawlish, looking at Trivett. 'We don't always get it right, do we?'

Trivett, who was strangely subdued, said quietly:

'What did Fowler do?'

'He just worked in with us,' said Simpson. 'Remember, the pay was good! He came here on the first housekeeper story, some months ago, and he joined us then. He warned us about you, Dawlish. Trivett being at your wedding and the mention of Terne for a honeymoon told him what was afoot.' He paused. 'Haven't I said enough?'

'Quite enough,' said Dawlish, slowly. 'Except—does the name "Cartwright" mean anything to you?'

Simpson looked blank. 'Why?' he asked.

'Just a red-herring,' murmured Dawlish.

There was not a great deal more to say, nor to do, for the fugitives had been well caught in North's trap.

'And so it happened and so it's ended,' Dawlish said, later. 'I've a few apologies to make and one or two meetings to attend, and then—we've two clear days left, Fel!'

'What about Sheila?' asked Felicity.

'Leave her to nurse Corbett, who by the way is doing very well,' said Dawlish. 'We've had three on this honeymoon long enough!'

It was the next morning before he and Felicity left Terne. Relaxed, happy, and at peace.

Two glorious days before them, they drove into the sun.

ABOUT THE AUTHOR

John Creasey, born in 1908, was a paramount English crime and science fiction writer who used myriad pseudonyms for more than six hundred novels. He founded the UK Crime Writers' Association in 1953. In 1962, his book *Gideon's Fire* received the Edgar Award for Best Novel from the Mystery Writers of America. Many of the characters featured in Creasey's titles became popular, including George Gideon of Scotland Yard, who was the basis for a subsequent television series and film. Creasey died in Salisbury, UK, in 1973.

THE PATRICK DAWLISH MYSTERIES

FROM OPEN ROAD MEDIA

OPEN ROAD

INTEGRATED MEDIA

Find a full list of our authors and
titles at www.openroadmedia.com

FOLLOW US
@OpenRoadMedia